THE PANDORA

PARTICLE

The Pandora Particle

By

Robert F. Orlando

DEDICATION

An individual can attain nothing without the support and encouragement of loved ones around them. In that spirit, I dedicate this work to the three people who most positively affected my life.

The first two are my parents, who interceded at an early age. My father taught me by example to be dedicated to my work and my family. He selflessly labored long hours to make certain his family had what it needed and that his son would be successful. My mother was the ever-present taskmaster that forced me to complete all my homework assignments. She provided discipline and an iron will.

The third person is my wife, Sue. She remains to this day both my harshest critic and my staunchest supporter. That is a task not easily managed but she performs it magnificently.

I appreciate these people for making me better and hope this novel honors them properly. Thanks to them, a person like me was able to create something that others may enjoy.

ABOUT THE AUTHOR

His love of travel, adventure and reading inspired this novel, his first literary achievement. Robert uses his many eclectic life experiences and vivid imagination to present his readers with fast-paced intrigue and mystery. He has a passion for the unexpected and ironic as evidenced within. A native of Philadelphia, he currently splits his time between Bucks County, Pennsylvania, and his beloved Hilton Head Island, South Carolina.

Table of Contents

Chapter 1 1

Chapter 2 4

Chapter 3 7

Chapter 4 13

Chapter 5 19

Chapter 6 24

Chapter 7 28

Chapter 8 32

Chapter 9 36

Chapter 10 42

Chapter 11 49

Chapter 12 53

Chapter 13 59

Chapter 14 63

Chapter 15 68

Chapter 16 72

Chapter 17 83

Chapter 18 87

Chapter 19 92

Chapter 20 96

Chapter 21 101

Chapter 22 107

Chapter 23 110

Chapter 24 114

Chapter 25 117

Chapter 26 121

Chapter 27 129

Chapter 28 132

Chapter 29 136

Chapter 30 141

Chapter 31 144

Chapter 32 149

Chapter 33 154

Chapter 34 166

Chapter 35 172

Chapter 36 177

Chapter 37 180

Chapter 38 190

Chapter 39 192

Chapter 40 195

Chapter 41 200

Chapter 42 202

Chapter 43 205

Chapter 44 207

Chapter 45 219

Chapter 46 222

Chapter 47 227

Chapter 48 230

Chapter 49 232

Chapter 50 235

Chapter 51 238

Chapter 52..242

Chapter 53..246

Chapter 54..258

Chapter 55..261

Chapter 1

Friday 11:00 PM, Fermi Lab. Batavia, IL

His eyes widen. A shuddering chill makes its way down his spine. The lab's systems are compromised. How long have they been watching? How much do they know? Fighting the mounting panic, he completes the diagnostics. The surveillance devices are super high-tech and foreign-made. He takes a deep breath and begins his efforts to block the signal. He knows that any success will be temporary and that they will overwrite his remedy in minutes, if not seconds. The window will be short, but it is the only solution.

Dr. Mark Stanton activates the temporary shield while simultaneously inserting the flash drive into his PC. The data is uploaded and ready for transmission. But to whom? His frayed mind can only think of one guaranteed safe location. Another lab is dared not risked…if they breach Fermi, no governmental facility is safe. He dreads what he is about to do but cannot conceive of an alternative. The upload finishes in seconds, and the send key is barely able to be pressed with his trembling hand.

The doctor now only has time for the briefest of messages to the recipient. Typing feverishly, he disengages moments before the intruders solve the blocking efforts and regain access to his machine.

Staring at the flash drive in an almost mesmerized state, he watches himself begin to destroy it and all the other traces of perhaps the greatest scientific discovery in history. A solitary prayer is whispered in the hope that this is indeed the right decision. The consequences of failure are too great to consider. The suddenness of the moment overwhelms him. His brain now comes to grips with the realization that they know he is aware of their presence. He gazes around the room at the remaining shift crew with paranoid uncertainty. There's no one he can trust.

Making a pretense to head to the restroom, he slips past the lavatory door and rushes from the building, heading for his car. Every noise is magnified, each echoing over the pounding of his heart. Navigating the dimly lit garage, he looks feverishly over his shoulder once, twice, and then for a third time. He searches for the ever-present specter of an imaginary assassin lurking in the shadows.

Unlocking the door of his white Camry, he sits in the driver's seat and closes his eyes. The awareness that he is now the target hits him like a palette of bricks. His brain is the only other vessel on earth containing this knowledge. That single fact makes the man both invaluable and expendable. The ignition is pressed, and the engine starts to rumble beneath the hood. The white sedan backs out of the parking space and races past the vacant security booth, tires screeching.

He exits the garage, turning west on Pine Street. Depressing the accelerator, his mind searches for a destination of refuge. With the knowledge that both his apartment in North Aurora and his fiancé in Chicago are off-limits, he decides to head for the Interstate, seeking safety in speed and distance. The gloom of solitude drapes over his seated figure as he races past the first intersection and makes a left turn on Kirk Road, heading south.

He is only minutes from I-88 and potentially safe territory. As the car approaches Butterfield Road, he notices the signal is red. The Toyota comes to a complete stop. Wet palms tightly grip the steering wheel. His breathing begins, returning slowly to near-normal patterns. Just then, he hears a large black SUV skid to a halt behind him. Through the mirror, he spies two dark-clad figures with automatic weapons to exit the vehicle and walk toward his car.

Still looking back, Mark slams his foot onto the gas pedal, and the tires spin. The car jerks forward. Entering the intersection, the vehicle is met broadside by a large semi racing east on Butterfield Road. The silence of the evening is broken by the sound of a deep-pitched horn before it is overtaken by crunching metal and a muted scream. The Camry and its only occupant are both rendered unrecognizable on impact. The brilliant scientist's time on earth ends suddenly.

The hunters rush back to their SUV and navigate past the wreckage continuing south on Kirk toward the highway.

Chapter 2

Saturday 6:00 AM, Butterfield Rd. and Kirk Rd., Aurora, IL

NSA investigators Diane Vitullo and Roger Edwards leaned against the side of her SUV. Confirmation of the car's ownership was now complete. Their worst fears were confirmed. Diane brushed her long, dark hair from her face as she pondered the multiple obstacles that lie before them.

The brightest and highest credentialed individual at Fermi Lab was either missing or dead. The partial clearance they were given to look at his file revealed that he headed up an extremely top-secret and very advanced research project. The details of this project were deemed too classified to be shared by the powers to be.

Diane's 5'9" frame ached from standing in the cold, windy night air, and so did that of her muscular partner. With high cheekbones and riveting brown eyes, she could have been a model. Fate, however, had her born into a long line of law enforcement officers. Her late parents were both FBI agents, having met on the job in their early twenties. They married and raised one daughter. Together, they instilled in her the genes and mindset of service.

Roger, on the other hand, was ex-military, serving in the Elite Green Berets for a decade. Slightly older than his partner, he maintained a fit body and a rugged handsomeness that endured into his forties. They worked well as a team and quickly became the government's go-to option for the most sensitive of cases.

They had been on the scene since 2:00 AM. The severity of the wreckage made the task of identification nearly impossible. The agency did have its resources, and they would be tested in this case. The driver's identity was still unknown, but with knowledge of the car's ownership, they could begin a preliminary investigation. She hated standing around doing nothing.

The first stop was to get to Mark Stanton's apartment in North Aurora. Sliding her sore feet back into her heels, Diane turned to her partner, and they quickly climbed into their vehicle. From all outward appearances, it looked like a normal Cadillac XT6. However, all agency cars are doctored after leaving the factory. This was no exception. She gunned the engine, and they sped off while Roger frantically dialed Dr. Stanton's cell phone, proffering the slimmest of hope it would be answered by him. A hurried voice message was left several attempts later, and communication efforts were terminated.

Heading west on Butterfield Rd., they made the 5.2-mile trip in less than thirteen minutes. Their trek had them snaking left, then right across the Fox River and onto S. Lincoln Highway north, turning east on Oak Street. Then a right on Randall until reaching Ritter St. Driving a bit further, they searched for the Randall Highlands Apartment complex. The sun was rising, and the night faded into memory.

As they approached the entrance to Apartment 1B24, they noticed pieces of wood on the ground and a busted doorjamb. They eyed each other, unholstered their weapons, and cautiously entered the apartment in the military fashion of trained agents. Both released the safety, preparing for the worst.

The unit was empty but in total disarray. It had been thoroughly and violently ransacked. The intruders were looking for something specific, and from the looks of it, they were unsuccessful. Both agents navigated past the mountains of overturned furniture and slashed bedding material. Piles of rumpled clothing and sharp ceramic chards littered the hardwood floor.

"We're too late," spouted agent Edwards, an obvious understatement.

Agent Vitullo focused her trained senses, intent on finding a lead within the chaos that lay before her. Looking down, she notices a birthday card in the rubble. It was a long shot, but this one proved promising. The card was from someone very close, his fiancé as the wording inside let on. The sender one Pamela Ward. A return address sticker was affixed to the envelope, and both agents intuitively knew their next move.

Without another word they made their way back out the front door and to the car. Roger entered the address into the GPS system on the dashboard, and the two drove forward. He followed by calling headquarters to request they send a team to secure the apartment. There was always the chance the intruders would return.

"Let's hope we beat them to the next site."

Chapter 3

Saturday 8:00 AM, Diversey Parkway, Printers Row, Chicago, IL

Pamela Ward awakens to the sound of soft music emanating from the bedside alarm of her Printers Row apartment situated at the corner of Diversey Parkway and Orchard Street. The rooms were furnished neatly with an eclectic pattern of furniture. Quaint but not overdone. Her head was slightly sore from a disappointing solo evening, which led to an excessive consumption of wine. She hated drinking alone.

Her long blonde hair is pulled back and tied. Pale skin reveals her Nordic heritage. Standing at 5'7", she gazes into the mirror and rubs her bright blue eyes. Her feet, clad in thick white socks, shuffled on the tiled floor. Gingerly, she rises from the bed, sleep reluctant to release her. A white robe is hung neatly on a hook near the queen-sized bed. First, she inserts her arms and then loosely ties the belt around her waist.

A quick glance at her cellphone's call and text logs proves negative. It seems like Mark never tried to contact her last night. A frown creases her lips. *He finally pulled an all-nighter*, she muses while stumbling into the kitchen to start brewing a large pot of coffee. She hoped the hot, dark liquid would revive her senses.

It was a cool September morning, and a breeze pushed soothing air onto the fourth-floor deck. Her lips enjoyed the warmth of the mug while the sounds of traffic whirred past on the street below. The news reporter on the radio made mention of a fatal crash last evening on Butterfield Rd. The ensuing fireball made the driver unrecognizable.

Her heart sagged momentarily, and she was ever so happy not to be at work in the Emergency Room of AMITA's St. Joseph's Hospital last evening. She was serving her internship there, tending to the injured and their loved ones. She longed to be in private practice, but for now, the job brought her close to Mark, and she would remain there until they at least set a date for the wedding.

The realization that her Saturday was planned for a lazy brunch with her fiancé, followed by a shopping excursion on the Magnificent Mile, made her smile. She admired his passion for lady science but rued its competition for the man she loved. Her knees rise into her chest, and she sips the remnants of her soothing black tonic with a smile, knowing she has him exclusively for the day. Life was indeed good.

Her laptop is fetched for pre-shopping reconnaissance before the decadent midday spree. With alarm she glares at the Outlook screen. An urgent message from Mark…*do not tell me he is cancelling*. Her distaste for lady science began to mushroom. She moves the cursor and clicks, totally unprepared for what happened next.

MY LOVE, THIS MESSAGE IS URGENT. I DON'T HAVE MUCH TIME. PLEASE LISTEN TO ME. YOUR SAFETY IS MY GREATEST CONCERN. I HAVE BEEN BOXED INTO A CORNER. SINISTER FORCES ARE AT WORK. YOU MUST DO THE FOLLOWING WITHOUT

DELAY. TRUST ME. I LOVE YOU MORE THAN ANYTHING IN THE WORLD:

FIRST YOU MUST DOWNLOAD THE ATTACHED FILE TO A FLASH DRIVE. THEN, BE SURE TO ERASE ALL OTHER COPIES. UNDER YOUR LAMP ON THE BEDROOM DRESSER IS A KEY, TAKE IT TO THE PNC BANK ON HALSTEAD AS SOON AS POSSIBLE. BRING YOUR LAPTOP. OPEN THE SAFETY DEPOSIT BOX.

YOU WILL LEARN MORE THERE, BUT I STRESS, YOU ARE NOT SAFE. LEAVE THE APARTMENT AS SOON AS POSSIBLE. I LOVE YOU SO MUCH AND MISS YOU ALREADY. I'M SO SORRY FOR INVOLVING YOU, BUT IT WAS MY ONLY OPTION. YOU ARE MY LIFE. PLEASE HEED THIS WARNING. I KNOW YOU CAN HANDLE THIS, AND WITH GOD'S GRACE, I'LL BE WITH YOU SOON. THIS IS NOT A JOKE. PLEASE DO AS I ASK.

Pamela's eyes stare at the screen and it seems like hours pass before she takes her next breath. Is this a joke or a bad dream? She races to the bedroom and lifts the lamp, startled to see a key taped to its bottom. *Holy shit, this is not a joke...*she rushes back to the laptop and begins to download the file while slipping into jeans and a knit top. Several minutes pass before the intense data dump finishes. Tugging on flats, she begins to erase everything and gather her belongings. The bank opens at 10:00 AM. If she hurries, she can be there when it does.

The apartment lies vacant for no more than twenty minutes when two black-clad figures pick the lock and deftly pass through the entrance. The duo is comprised of a male and a female both of Asian origin, with dark hair and yellow to olive complexion. The male known as Chen Zhao was a long-time member of the Tong before selling his services to the highest bidder. He stands at 5'7 with a solid frame. He is known for his ruthless aggression.

The female was a Chinese Intelligence Officer before giving way to more capitalistic ideals. She measures in at 5'5 and calls herself Jun Li. She is an expert in martial arts. Their black garb conceals most of their bodies and a portion of their face. A homage to the ninja warriors of the past. Thin and athletic, they make no wasted movements and begin their intense and disruptive search. The once neat domain transforms into one of chaos. Moving quickly and trained as a team, their efficiency is amazing…in minutes, the apartment is completely laid bare. If it had held any secrets, they would have been discovered without a doubt.

Three unanswered calls have Agent Edwards discarding his phone in utter frustration as the Cadillac navigates from North Aurora to Printers Row. The 46-mile ride seemed like an eternity. One hour later they pull onto Orchard Rd. and into the garage. Locating the elevator, they hastily board and press FOUR on the keypad. Their hearts beat rapidly, exaggerating the delay.

Finally, the doors open, and they stride with purpose toward the apartment. The frustrated intruders are preparing to leave when they hear the elevator doors followed by racing footsteps in the hallway. Someone is approaching quickly. Without a word, each moved to a strategic location within the room, silently prepared for whatever played out.

The agents knocked on the door several times, unwittingly allowing more time for the ambushers to ready themselves.

As the repeated raps go unanswered, Diane decides to dispense with the protocol of a warrant and gain entry. Alarms inside them ring when they realize the door latch is not locked. Without a word, weapons are gripped. Agent Edwards turns the handle while Vitullo prepares to rush forward firearm extended.

On the second of her two hurried paces into the room, a foot appears out of nowhere, knocking the Glock pistol out of her hands. The agent turns quickly, but her enemy is prepared and sends a perfectly executed straight kick, landing squarely on her chin. Dianes' head snaps back, and she stumbles in reverse, losing one of her heels. She kicks off the other and responds with two hard punches thrown in rapid succession. They are both deftly dodged and hit only air.

Another well-placed kick causes an explosion in her ribcage, doubling over her tall frame and eliciting a torrent of warm air from her gaping mouth. Fighting feverishly, she grabs at the black material adorning her foe and blindly tugs as hard as she can. That's when she feels two palms on the back of her head, forcing it downward into a rising knee. A flash of white is the last thing she sees before crumpling to the floor unconscious.

On the opposite side of the apartment, Agent Edwards has the other intruder securely trapped in a chokehold on the floor. In seconds, he will be out. Unfortunately, now rid of the opposition, Jun Li is free to assist. She grabs an overturned lamp and slams it into the back of Roger's head, stunning him and voiding his grip. Both assassins flee quickly, leaving the two NSA agents lying on the floor dazed and a bit humbled.

Chapter 4

Saturday 10:00AM, PNC Bank, 2600 N. Halstead St., Chicago, IL

Pamela Ward arrived just before the bank opened, so she walked past the entrance and down to the corner of W. Wrightwood Ave. Seeing this served to kill as much time as necessary she turns back and enters just as the manager is unlocking the front door. She presents her ID and the key she had retrieved from under the lamp. The bank officer leads her to the private room reserved solely for this purpose. He removes the large metal box from the wall and politely exits. The shaken blonde is trembling so severely that she has difficulty fitting the small key into the lockset. Using both hands, she finally manages to open the lid. Gazing inside her very existence is challenged.

She peers into the box and sees a large amount of cash piled in stacks. There were groups of various denominations ranging from five to one hundred dollars. Lying adjacent to the cash were two sets of passports and driver's licenses. Her picture and that of her fiancé appear on them. However, the names and addresses are different for each. The site of his photograph sends a sharp pang to her heart. She also spies two sets of credit cards from different banks with names matching those on the passports and licenses. Her chest tightens, and she struggles to breathe. *What the hell am I involved in, and how long was he planning this?* There is also an envelope containing another flash drive.

It was marked with the following:

"IMPORTANT… PLAY THIS MY LOVE."

She fumbles but inserts the flash stick into her laptop and clicks on the only file it contains. A video begins. The weary visage of her fiancé appears in a dimly lit room. He looks like he hasn't slept in weeks. He begins to speak.

DEAREST PAM, IF YOU ARE WATCHING THIS VIDEO, MY WORST FEARS HAVE COME TRUE. I AM EITHER IN HIDING OR WORSE AND CANNOT COME TO YOU. YOU ARE IN GREAT DANGER BECAUSE OF ME AND MY WORK.

FOR THAT, I AM TRULY SORRY. BUT YOU ALSO HAVE THE POWER TO SAVE US, OUR COUNTRY AND PERHAPS OUR WORLD. I'LL DO MY BEST TO EXPLAIN. IN THE EVER-PRESENT SEARCH TO IMPROVE ENERGY EFFICIENCY, I EMBARKED ON AN ATTEMPT TO USE HARMONICS TO CREATE A FRACTIONAL QUANTUM HALL EFFECT AT OR NEAR ROOM TEMPERATURE. THE RESONANCE WAS USED TO ENHANCE THE TRANSFORMATION OF MATTER INTO A TWO-DIMENSIONAL OR FLATLAND STATE. AT LEAST, THAT'S WHAT WE THOUGHT. AT FIRST, THE PROCESS LASTED ONLY SECONDS, AND EVERYTHING RETURNED TO ITS NORMAL CONDITION. WHEN WE ADDED MORE POWER AND MODIFIED THE ALGORITHMS, WE WERE ABLE TO EXTEND THE TRANSFORMATION TIME.

AT A CERTAIN POINT, WHEN THE MATTER RETURNED TO OUR THREE-DIMENSIONAL REALITY, IT WAS ALTERED PERMANENTLY. IT TRANSFIGURED

INTO STRANGE HYPERDIMENTIONAL PARTICLES OF EQUAL MASS. THIS MATERIAL, ALTHOUGH HAVING ALL THE ATTRIBUTES OF A SOLID, WAS COMPRISED OF PURE ENERGY. WE ARE STILL NOT CERTAIN WHAT IS HAPPENING. WE NAMED IT THE PANDORA PARTICLE. IN THE RIGHT HANDS, AN OUNCE OF THIS SUBSTANCE COULD POWER THE ENTIRE CITY OF CHICAGO FOR A YEAR. IN THE WRONG, A TABLESPOON COULD ANNIHILATE ILLINOIS IN SECONDS.

THEN THE MILITARY CAME IN AND ASSERTED CONTROL. OUR TEAM FELT IT WAS ESSENTIAL TO PAUSE AND INVESTIGATE THE FUNDAMENTAL CHANGES TO THE OBJECTS AND THE PROPERTIES OF THIS ODD MATERIAL. MY RECOMMENDATION WAS TO CEASE ALL EXPERIMENTATION UNTIL MORE DATA WAS COLLECTED, BUT I WAS OVERRULED. WEAPONIZATION WAS THEIR ONLY CONCERN. THEY SOUGHT TO OBTAIN AS MUCH EXOTIC MATERIAL AS THEY COULD AS QUICKLY AS POSSIBLE. I ALSO DISCOVERED AN ATTEMPT TO STEAL SOME OF THIS STRANGE SUBSTANCE AND QUICKLY CLASSIFIED AND CATALOGUED OUR RESULTS.

AS A RESULT OF ALL THIS HARMONIC ACTIVITY AND FOCUSED ENERGY, SOME KIND OF TEAR OR RIPPLE IN SPACE APPEARED. I FEAR IT IS UNSTABLE. THE GAP IN BETWEEN THE MATTER IN ITS TWO- AND THREE-DIMENSIONAL STATES NEVER CLOSED. IT WAS THEN THAT I DECIDED TO TAKE

DRASTIC MEASURES. THE PLAN YOU ARE NOW WITNESSING WAS FORMED.

I ERASED ALL TRACES OF THE PROGRAM. THE COPY ON YOUR FLASH DRIVE IS THE ONLY ONE THAT EXISTS. TO MAKE MATTERS WORSE, I DISCOVERED WE HAD BEEN INFILTRATED BY A THIRD PARTY.

THAT'S WHEN I KNEW I COULDN'T JOIN YOU. THERE IS LITTLE DOUBT THEY WILL BE HUNTING FOR ME. I AM SO DEEPLY SORRY, BUT I SAW YOU AS THE ONLY CONDUIT TO GET THIS INFORMATION TO ONE PERSON WITH THE KNOWLEDGE AND THE POWER TO FIX IT. YOU, MY LOVE, ARE THE ONLY ONE I COULD TRUST TO REACH HIM. PLEASE USE THE TOOLS I HAVE LEFT HERE FOR YOU AND GET BOTH FLASH DRIVES TO DR. CAMERON ALLEN AT THE SMITHSONIAN INSTITUTE IN WASHINGTON, DC.

DO NOT GO BACK TO THE APARTMENT UNDER ANY CIRCUMSTANCE, AND PLEASE BE CAREFUL. DON'T FLY DIRECTLY FROM O'HARE. RENT A CAR, DRIVE TO MILWAUKEE AND LEAVE FROM THERE. IT IS IMPERATIVE YOU GET TO HIM BEFORE THEY FIND YOU. I WAS HOPING TO MAKE THIS JOURNEY WITH YOU, BUT FATE DICTATED OTHERWISE.

I LOVE YOU AND ALWAYS WILL. PLEASE BE CAREFUL, I COULDN'T BEAR THE THOUGHT OF ANYTHING HAPPENING TO YOU.

She awoke this morning as a blissful young bride-to-be planning a shopping excursion. In the short time since, she finds herself on the run, hiding from killers and immersed in a plot to save the world. Is this really happening? She stares at the blank screen, unable to move. But move she must.

A bleary-eyed and numb young intern stumbles her way into a passing CitiCab taxi. Her apartment is now inaccessible, so her brain scurries to find a destination. The driver impatiently awaits her decision. She requests him to take her to the W Hotel on Adams Street. She and Mark had spent a wonderful weekend there when they first met.

Refuge is now being sought in the past. Pam loses herself in thought as the cab makes its way east on Fullerton before turning south on Lakeshore Dr. They exit on Jackson Drive West, jogging north up onto Adams. The ride, which is less than six miles, takes over 20 minutes, but the passenger doesn't seem to mind. She drifts off in the backseat, trying to digest everything she has been fed this morning. The fare is paid in cash, and a confused young woman leaves the cab, walking trance-like through the entrance and toward the front desk.

With the fake ID, she checks into the familiar suite, trying to cling to happier times. Dragging herself into the elevator, she presses the proper floor leading up to her residence for the evening. She enters the room and collapses onto the bed, sobbing. Her frayed nerves finally snap. Longing for sleep, she hopes the darkness can soothe the aching in her soul.

But as she closes her eyes, she remembers the look on Mark's face and the dire warning from the video. There's way too much work to do. Perhaps more than she can handle in her fragile state. Finding some solace in her mission, a search is initiated on her laptop. Flights from Milwaukee to Washington, DC, are scrutinized, and she discovers a daily excursion departing General Mitchell Airport each day at 1:23 PM and arriving at Reagan National at 4:28 PM. A first-class ticket is purchased in her new persona, Vanessa Redfield. She pays with a credit card of the same name. Next, she looks for a rental car and finds an Enterprise Rental facility on Madison Avenue. It is within walking distance. Busying herself seems to be the best cure for her anxiety and depression. When all these details are finalized, she collapses onto the large bed. Unable to sleep, she spends the night staring at the ceiling, caressing the only remaining photograph of the love of her life.

How could things change so drastically in such a short time? The world she awoke to only hours before no longer existed.

Chapter 5

Saturday 4:00 PM, NSA Headquarters, Undisclosed location, Chicago, IL

The NSA's (National Security Agency) office in Chicago is small by any measurable standards. It houses a dozen agents and twice as many analysts and support staff. They operate in anonymity. There are no signs and the entry on the directory simply reads SUITE 1100. You must know how to find them. Although the agency has been in existence in some form or another since the beginning of the Cold War, it never received much attention or funding until the Twin Towers fell on September 11, 2001. Its chief purpose was anti-terrorism, but it was also called upon when the dividing lines between the CIA and FBI became blurred. They can act independently and in a freer manner. Their agents are all elite highly trained individuals skilled mentally and physically.

Diane holds an ice pack on her swollen and slightly discolored cheekbone. Her jaw and ribs still ache but far less than the sting of good-natured comments levied by her fellow agents. She grins, taking all in stride but longing to even the score with the bitch that ambushed her. The ice causes her to wince while her partner peruses the latest information that was recently added to Dr. Stanton's dossier.

The office that day had two such agents desperately trying to make sense of the bizarre events at Fermi Lab. But how could they make any progress without the vital information that was being withheld? Why was Ward's apartment searched? What were they seeking? Why is the experiment, now on hold, still deemed classified? Crucial knowledge relevant to it and the experimenter was intentionally being withheld. They needed to know a lot more if they were going to be successful. Even their attackers seemed better informed. Something extremely specific was being sought in each of the two apartments. Something so valuable was erased from the record.

By this time, it had been confirmed that Dr. Stanton was the occupant of the Camry, meeting his untimely demise on Butterfield Rd. All efforts were now being made to keep this from the press. She placed another call to Fermi Lab requesting to speak with Colonel Fielding, the man who was now in control of the project. Her efforts were once again dodged, and she was forced to leave a third message. Diane was not accustomed to being ignored. It made the agent's temperature rise above its boiling point. Roger noticed this and threw the file he was holding at her with the hope that he could diffuse the mounting tempest. He also offered to reach out to his old army contacts to see if he could turn up anything. It seems ten years of exemplary service in the Green Berets still garnered respect in most circles.

Roger was, in every sense of the word, a hero. Through two tours in the Middle East, he displayed courage and intelligence rarely found in one individual. As a special forces officer, he earned several medals for bravery and decisiveness in action. The man never displayed or discussed them. The agent was also well-spoken and polished, an even rarer combination. His dedication to the job was matched by a dedication to his body. He routinely engaged in rigorous workouts whose results were evident even under his long-sleeved shirts.

By tapping his network, Roger was able to gather the following: Dr. Mark Stanton had taken something from the lab. It was not in the vehicle at the time of the accident. The project he headed was on indefinite hold due to complications from the above.

While helpful, the agents were still left with the daunting task of figuring this whole mess out. The added information was entered on their whiteboard. They quickly deduced that the Asian duo they had encountered had been sent to find whatever was taken from the lab. The death of Stanton made this object more critical. They needed to achieve two short-term goals:

> Find Pamela Ward
> Gain a back door into Fermi Lab.

Desperate for another lead, Diane noticed in the file that Stanton maintained a joint bank account with his fiancé at the PNC Bank at 2600 Halstead, just two blocks from Ward's apartment. Calls were made to high-level management, and with a little arm twisting, it was learned that Ms. Ward entered the bank this morning. Under pressure, management agreed that they would open the branch on Sunday at 10:00 AM to allow for inspection and interviews.

Locating Ms. Ward was now increased to priority one. It necessitated a watch on all airports and Train Stations within a 60-mile radius. A mild debate as to whether to publicize the search and show her photo on TV ensued, with the negative prevailing. Units were then dispatched to stake out both apartments in the unlikely event she or anyone returned.

With the preceding preparations made, Diane offered to drive her partner home and pick him up the following morning. It was a long day. Both welcomed a hot shower and a good night's sleep. A weary agent parked the Cadillac and entered her two-bedroom apartment. She moved into the Mode Building off Armitage at Campbell Avenue two years ago. She always dressed in her "uniform," as she would like to call it, consisting of a blazer, a skirt, a button-down top, and pantyhose. She kicked off her mid-heel pumps and removed her jacket…still clad in in the remaining garments. She then removes her gun and holster and folds her long legs under her on the sofa.

The day was long, frustrating, and somewhat painful. She gazes at the plaque her mom gave her on her sixteenth birthday, the last they would celebrate together. Displayed prominently on her wall was the following:

"Doing what you love is freedom. Loving what you do is happiness."

-Lana Del Rey

Diane thought about those words every day. They provided support and motivation. She so loved police work and her rise to lead detective in the NSA was meteoric. Her parents were career FBI and true role models. Both were her heroes. They met on the job and instantly fell madly in love, remaining in that state until their untimely demise at the hands of a mugger. It happened just as Diane was approaching her seventeenth birthday. They were brutally assaulted returning home from a dinner celebrating her Uncle Trevor's appointment as Deputy Director of the CIA. Things like that were not supposed to happen on the upscale sidewalks of Georgetown.

In her early life, she worked feverishly to please them and, after their death, vowed to find the killer. Rendered a teenage orphan, she was raised by her uncle and achieved student-scholar status throughout her four years of college at Georgetown University. She lettered in both lacrosse and field hockey. An only child, she inherited the instincts of a sleuth with an athletic body and stunning looks. It was both a blessing and a curse. Uncle Trevor undoubtedly aided her career and her ultimate acceptance into the NSA, but her achievements thereafter were all based on merit. His decision to transfer her to Chicago at first rebuked, and minimized any internal talk of favoritism. Diane was respected by all her coworkers but didn't date much. Her suspicious nature was always sabotaging potential suitors, and ever-present in her mind was the obligation to find the cold-blooded murderer(s) that robbed her of her beloved parents.

She sat and gazed at the blank TV screen. What was she missing in this case? Why does a well-respected scientist risk all to sabotage his own project? And why now? Furthermore, if what they suspect is true, why does he involve the woman he loves and change her life? With these thoughts bubbling to a froth in her brain, the exhausted detectives' eyes glaze, and she succumbs to a much too delayed slumber.

Chapter 6

Saturday 8:00 PM, Penthouse ParTec Industries, Old Dominion Drive & Lowell Ave, McLean, VA

The CEO of ParTec Industries, Daniel Dryden, is seated at his desk in the opulent penthouse office on Old Dominion Ave. His CFO and sister, Kristen, is sitting by his side in a visitor's chair, her ever-present gym bag lying next to her seat. Daniel is the perfect picture of the modern executive in a navy sportscoat, khaki pants, and a tieless shirt opened at the collar. Kristen, on the other hand, while attractive and feminine, looks more muscular and athletic. Daniel's pale complexion and thinning hair are the opposite of Kristen's tanned skin and thick auburn mane. Both are gazing at the wall-sized monitor flickering to life across the room.

The siblings inherited the company from their parents, who forged a great working relationship with the right high-level U.S. security officials. As successors, they tried their best to maintain their usefulness to the powers-to-be. They were astute enough to know most of their income was government-sourced and of questionable legality, so they didn't ask any questions. Breaking the rules was part of the game as was the hiring of mercenaries when necessary.

At first, static covers the screen, but soon, it clears, revealing the faces of Chen Zhao and Jun Li as they appear to be sitting in a dull, nondescript room. A stark contrast in settings. Daniel, brimming with brash confidence, is clearly in charge and speaks first. "We would like a status report on

24

the assignment. Our patience is being tested as we await an update on your efforts."

Both agents are clad in tight-fitting t-shirts. Dark tights adorn Jun's shapely legs while Chen's are covered in black slacks. The absence of material displays their lean but muscular torsos. A scowl appears on Jun's face, and Chen quickly takes the lead and responds.

"The target discovered our devices Friday evening at 2300 hours. He was somehow able to jam our signal for several minutes using some kind of sophisticated magnetic pulse. Fortunately, we were able to devise countermeasures, and as the pulse weakened, our surveillance resumed. All systems are currently active, and we are continuously monitoring the laboratory. At this time, all work on the project has been halted. When transmission resumed only minutes later, the target was located packing his briefcase and heading for the exit. We believe he used this time to transmit the information to another party. Jun and I were not far from the premises, and we chose to pursue and apprehend. We did not see his vehicle until we were behind it. It was moving south on Kirk Rd. Whereupon he came to a stop at the light on Butterfield. We exited our SUV and were about to capture the target when he spotted us in the rear view mirror. He sped forward without looking. Halfway through the intersection, he was met broadside by a speeding truck. The car was destroyed on impact, and the truck driver immediately used his cell phone to contact the authorities. Our scanner picked up the presence of a police cruiser nearby, so we thought it was best to flee the scene."

"Our assessment of the collision was that the target could not have survived. The twisted metal ignited, and if anything was inside, the flames would render it useless."

"It was then we decided to implement plan B and get a look inside the target's apartment. We found nothing inside, but we learned that he had a fiancé living in Chicago. We arrived at her empty flat late in the morning and proceeded to search through it as well with the same result. However, as we were about to exit, two government agents entered the room, and we were forced to neutralize them."

A scowl on Dryden's face openly displays his disappointment at the summation. His response is cold, emotionless, but chilling, nonetheless.

"I pay you handsomely, and I expect the results to be commensurate with that compensation. You have wasted my time with excuses, and we have gained nothing. Furthermore, you were nearly discovered. How do you expect me to react?"

There is an exaggerated silence spanning several seconds until Jun Li responds.

"We will find the girl first, but failing that, we have an insurance policy. I placed a tracking device in the tall agent's holster after I rendered her unconscious. If they find her before us, we will be right behind."

Dryden musters a small smile, impressed by the female assassin.

"Clever move, Ms. Li, but do not disappoint me. The stakes are high for all of us."

With that, he abruptly terminates the conversation. Daniel and Kristen begin to converse when the computer announces an income transmission. Both turn to stare at the screen. This time there is no video and no sound. The following appears on the screen:

DANIEL, DO YOU HAVE THE INFORMATION I SEEK?

Daniel's demeanor shrinks from one of stern confidence to that of subservience. Kristen's expression remains stoic. He nervously tries to clear his throat and type in, NOT YET, SIR, BUT…

His typing ceases when the next line appears:

DO NOT FAIL ME, DANIEL DRYDEN. YOU WON'T LIKE THE CONSQUENCES.

The screen returns to black; the sister exchanges a long look with her now pale brother. With Stanton dead, there is only one source left for them to obtain the information they are in desperate need of. They dare not think of the consequences should someone else get it first.

Chapter 7

Sunday 6:00 AM, Fermi Lab., Batavia, IL

The timing of this meeting was intended to send a dual message to the remaining scientists. First and foremost, it was to emphasize his ultimate power and total control over them. This served his inflated ego as much as the task at hand. Second, it was to drive home the importance of finding a rapid solution. The Colonel made promises to deliver ample quantities of this highly sought-after exotic material, and he always kept his promises. His 6'3" frame was garbed in a finely creased olive uniform adorned with medals and ribbons earned throughout his illustrious career. The gray of his closely cropped hair battled for control with the remaining dark brown strands. His taut skin belied his age, which was now well into his late fifties.

Holding his hat under his arm, he stands, allowing the silence to unnerve the frail pencil pushers before him. He loathed weakness. These snowflakes were treating paper cuts while he was learning to stay alive in Iraq.

After a lengthy pause he begins with a question. From his training days at West Point Military Academy, he always favored a frontal assault. "Does anyone care to tell me what this enigma is and why we cannot transmit more material?" The room remained silent. The current staff was comprised of experimental physicists who were less inclined to posit theory. Trembling, most were reluctant to even make eye contact. Fearing rebuke, a slender man with a balding head and thick glasses raised his hand.

With the stern eyes of the Colonel bearing down on him, he states, "Sir, we believe it is a ripple created by the wave effect of transitional matter." The comment is met with a scowl and a derisive, "A ripple but a ripple in what, Einstein?"

Another hand rises, and a young woman in a white lab coat blurts out, "Space, sir, the matter shrunk a dimension too rapidly for the void to be filled naturally."

It is quickly followed by a male voice yelling, "It could be time as well."

Then, a third mumbling, "Space-time." Unsatisfied, he turns to Dr. Stanton's second-in-command and now temporary team leader, Dr. Stephanie Millstead.

"Colonel, I believe what we have is a vacuum in the fabric of reality itself. All our tests have failed to provide any answers. Our instruments stopped working in the void. Inside it, matter and energy obey different laws if they obey any. Furthermore, while it is stable in size for now, it is growing in intensity."

Her remarks met with a response she could not answer. "How can **nothing** grow in intensity?"

Sarah knew when to retreat, and she sat back down. "We just don't know, sir. It's just that the pulse rate has increased substantially, which is why I recommended that we cease all transmissions when the anomaly formed."

Her statement was quickly rebuffed. "Dr. Millstead, please do not let me have to remind you again. You're here to supply information, not formulate policy. Is that clear?"

The learned doctor could only muster a red-faced nod and look away.

"Now listen up. I want people working on this 24/7. Nobody has a day off until we can start transmitting again. Do whatever is necessary to control this thing as quickly as possible. I am having additional experts flown in from out west next week on military planes to assist. I want answers. Failure is not an option. Dismissed."

The Colonel exits the room and makes a point to walk past the containment room on his departure. Peering into the window, he pauses momentarily and ponders. What the hell are you, and where did you come from? Resuming his trek back into his temporary office, he sits back in his chair. He loved authority. Reacting to the beep on his laptop he presses in a code. On the screen, against a black backdrop, these words appear.

COLONEL, WHAT HAVE YOU LEARNED?

His breathing halts as he fumbles to formulate a coherent response, typing in:

NO ANSWERS YET, BUT WE BELIEVE THAT WE ARE CLOSE. I'LL NEED SOME MORE TIME TO BE CERTAIN WE CAN RESUME.

Several seconds pass, and:

HOW MUCH TIME DO YOU NEED TO PRODUCE MORE OF THE PARTICLES?

Fumbling with the keyboard, the Colonel enters:

A WEEK OR TWO AT THE MOST.

An immediate reply appears:

GOOD, DO NOT DISAPPOINT ME, MARSHALL. I TRUST THAT I DO NOT HAVE TO REMIND YOU WHAT IS AT STAKE. YOU WERE PUT HERE TO DO A JOB, AND WE EXPECT IT TO BE DONE QUICKLY.

A bead of perspiration rolls down the brow of one Marshall Fielding, Colonel United States Army.

Chapter 8

Sunday 7:00 AM, W Hotel Adams Street, Chicago, IL

Pamela tosses and turns in the king-sized bed of her luxurious suite. She is awake well before the alarm begins to buzz. A night of restless sleep has done little to mend her frayed nerves. Her body numbly rises, and she begins donning the hotel robe. The frantic tone of Mark's voice in the video reminding her she must leave town replays over and over in her head.

A knock on the door signals the room service cart has arrived, and she welcomes the hot breakfast thereon, quickly devouring a mushroom omelet. The waiter was generously tipped and left a second pot of coffee. The warm brew is used to wash everything down. It soothes and gives her a bit of energy.

Foremost in her mind is to get to the rental car and drive north to Wisconsin as quickly as possible. The warning Mark left was serious. She replays the message over and over in her head. Each time feeling the strain in his voice. Her unknown pursuers must be both serious and vicious people. A quick inventory of her limited possessions takes little to no time. There are some items she must acquire to begin this journey. Having hurriedly left the apartment, she only took what she was wearing. She makes a list in her mind and, after a quick shower, dons the only clothing available. That will have to change.

She stops at the front desk to return the key to the very amiable hotel clerk, asking what time the shops open. Pam is disappointed to hear "Ten AM on Sunday."

Responding with a "Thank you," she exits into the brisk morning air. "What a lovely day for a stroll."

On foot, she walks west from Adams to Wells and turns right, proceeding north until reaching Madison. At the corner, she can see the green Enterprise Car Rental sign.

A left turn takes her to 201 West Madison, and she is greeted by an athletic young man at precisely 8:00 AM, stating her reservation is in order. The youth can't help but stare into her saucer-shaped blue eyes. She decides a mild flirtation is in order.

He stammers awkwardly, "A week rental. Are you going on a trip?"

She bats her eyes and tells him she is visiting family in Indiana and will be very bored.

"I wish you could come."

A beet-red blush covers his face. "Me Too."

The non-descript sedan she had selected rolls to the pickup point, and they perform the standard walk around. They note the small dent on the rear passenger side panel, and the keys are handed off. At approximately 8:45, she drives out of the garage and finds the onramp for I-90 North. A part of her wonders if she will ever see Chicago again. Her Ford merges onto I-94 at the junction and remains on it until leaving Illinois in the rear-view mirror. Nearing Milwaukee, she sees road signs directing traffic to General Mitchell Airport, and she takes Route 119 towards it. But something in her head tells her to turn off onto Route 38, where she drives south. She remembers from a spy movie never to park at the airport. The car keeps moving until she notices the Hilton Garden Inn on the left-hand side and pulls into the parking lot, proceeding directly to an inconspicuous space behind the building. This will take them longer to find. Abandoning the car, she hops onto the airport shuttle for the seven-minute ride to the terminal.

With minimum Sunday activity, she sifts through security quickly and has some time to purchase a small travel bag, some necessary toiletries, makeup, and additional clothing, topping everything off with a Brewers baseball cap and a pair of large sunglasses. Fully supplied, she makes her way to the gate at 12:30, where she busies herself with the Sunday paper until she is called to board. The flight departs on time at 1:23 PM. The destination is Ronald Reagan International Airport, Washington, DC.

A flight attendant offers a beverage, and she responds with, "White wine, please."

Sitting in an empty first-class cabin, she closes her eyes for a brief nap. Her mind drifts off to happier times, romantic dinners, old movies, and wedding plans. Although asleep, a tear still forms and rolls down her pale cheek. How did she end up here?

The uneventful two-hour flight arrives only slightly past the 4:28 arrival time. Everything is pretty much routine for the crew, and all the passengers save one. Exiting into the terminal, a chill rippled down her spine. She realizes how long it's been since she has been in the Nation's Capital. Making her way to the cab stand, she utters the well-rehearsed destination,

"Waldorf Astoria, 1100 Pennsylvania Ave., please."

The taxi enters the freeway and takes I-395 to the 12th Street Expressway, exiting at 12th Street and pulling into the extravagant entrance, where she is greeted by a burly doorman who opens her door and offers to take her bags. With minimum luggage, she graciously declines, pays the fare, and ambles trancelike into this quasi-palace, hoping there is a room available. At the front desk, she checks in using the same alternate ID but pays upfront with cash, knowing the credit card can be traced.

She is handed the keys to a lavish room on the fifth floor and heads for the elevators. Sitting on the bed, she feels the pangs of hunger once more. Another room service meal is ordered. To guarantee sleep, she adds a large bottle of pinot grigio. Her only goal tonight is to rest.

Chapter 9

Sunday 10:00AM, PNC Bank, 2600 N. Halstead St., Chicago, IL

The Manager and every employee who worked on Saturday were ordered to return on Sunday morning for some urgent government business. Roger Edwards circulated around the office, distributing a questionnaire to each attendee. Aside from the normal profile information, the form also required them to provide a description of the target, explain in detail any interaction, and provide a map of where in the office they worked or encountered Customer X. Diane was in the manager's office finishing his interview and prepping it for the interrogations to follow. A forensic team was already in place scouring the safety deposit room for any clues that may have been left.

The employees were understandably annoyed and intimidated by the proceedings. A firm but delicate touch was needed to alleviate the fear and assure maximum cooperation. She started every interview by emphasizing to each party that they were not in any legal jeopardy. In private, each was asked to describe the blonde customer and to relay in detail any interaction they may have had. The questions were scientifically designed to promote recall and, combined with Diane's training as an interviewer, bolstered the odds of success.

One by one, each was paraded into the office. It was becoming clear that most of the employees were oblivious to anything of any importance. Frustration was setting in. The last potential witness, a menial receptionist, offered two-word answers between loud cracks of gum. Wearily, Diane rose set to terminate the proceedings without any progress when the position of the reception desk at the bank window was spotted.

A quick turn and, "When she left the bank, did you see where she went?"

Her heart stops when the young girl utters,

"UHH HUH, she got into a cab right there."

A follow-up is quickly posited.

"Did you get the name of the cab company...?"

"It was the yellow and green kind... Citi something."

At last, their first lead. The tall agent was reinvigorated, motioning madly for Roger to retrieve the car while she searched for the address of Citi Cab's closest facility on her phone. She begged a forensic team member to handle the exit procedures and raced for the door. Not waiting for the car to come to a complete stop, she climbs into the passenger seat and yells 2601 W. Peterson. A lifelong citizen of Chicago, Roger doesn't need GPS to recognize the location. He makes a hard U-turn on Halstead and revs the engine heading north. A screeching turn east on Belmont and then Lake Shore Drive north. Light Sunday traffic and deft driving help to reduce the trip time from the normal 30 minutes to 23 minutes flat.

Diane dialed the cab company, making certain someone was prepared for their arrival. The Weekend dispatcher said he would meet them in the office and search his records for anything that might help. The speeding Cadilac came to a sudden stop at the office door, and the agents disembarked, determined to make this opportunity count.

Flashing their badges, they backed the middle-aged man to his desk. They demanded to know who picked up a fare near the PNC Bank on Halstead yesterday afternoon. Forceful yet polite, the detectives made it known that it was in his best interest to comply. Without hesitation, he offered the driver's name. Hassan Bajani was identified, and the agents demanded an interview with him.

"He is out on the road. His shift doesn't end until 6:00 PM."

Roger gripped the man's arm ever so slightly to emphasize the request was not optional. A radio dispatch was immediately sent out, ordering him to return to the garage. The cab reaches the garage at precisely 2:05 PM, and the driver is met by the trio holding a large photograph of their blonde quarry.

"Do you remember picking this woman up near the PNC bank on Halstead yesterday?"

Hassan hesitates a second, and Roger leans inward and places his muscled arm on the man's shoulder to assist with the recall. "Sir?"

"Ugh, yes, I remember."

"Where did you take her?" Diane growls from several paces away.

"I drove her to the W Hotel on Adams Street."

"Did she say anything else?"

"No, miss, she wasn't much of a talker."

Roger's hand slides from the man's shoulder, and in unison, both agents turn and break into a trot headed back to the vehicle with Diane ceding the driver's seat to her partner. Destination: The W Hotel.

At roughly 2:45 PM Sunday afternoon, the serenity of the W Hotel main entrance is disrupted by a speeding vehicle coming to an abrupt stop at the valet desk. Badges are flashed without a word, and the duo races past the doorman to the front desk.

The perky desk clerk looks up at Diane and her shield with apprehension.

"Do you have a guest registered here named Pamela Ward?"

A brief scan of the register reveals no one by that name.

"No, ma'am, not for the last several days," squeaks from the clerk's mouth.

Diane flashes the photo and there is instant recognition.

"Oh, her, that is Vanessa Redfield. She stayed in a suite last night and checked out early this morning."

Roger walks around the desk to obtain copies of the required driver's license and credit card that were placed on file.

"I'll run this through to see where it's been used."

The clerk is trembling, "Am I in any trouble?"

Diane eases her concern, "No, dear, but this is very important government business. Can you tell me anything she said or where she was headed?"

"No, ma'am. But she left on foot because she said it was a lovely day for a stroll."

Roger returns with the results of the credit card activity.

"Three transactions: W Hotel, Enterprise Car Rental, and American Airlines."

They find the Enterprise location minutes away and head straight there while Diane attempts to contact American Airlines to find out the destination of the ticket "Vanessa" purchased. After several minutes of discussion with the smitten rental car youth they quickly determined the Indiana story was a smoke screen. Our target fled somewhere by air, but where...every second of delay lessened their chances of success.

The long Sunday finally comes to an end with the agents anxiously awaiting more information. Both head back to their respective apartments where they receive word that American Airlines has replied.

The card was used for a one-way ticket from General Mitchell Airport in Milwaukee to Ronald Reagan International Airport in Washington, DC. Diane immediately knows what she must do. Make the trip to DC, and while there, attempt to enlist the aid of the only ally who has the power to pull some strings at Fermi. She contacts the District Police Department to advise them of her arrival and requests their aid with the search. She then places a private call. Tickets are booked for a Monday morning flight from O'Hare, and a dinner meeting in McLean, VA, is planned. Reuniting with family is always a pleasure, but this dinner will hopefully serve another purpose.

Diane had only good memories of her uncle. He was there for her in her darkest moments. When her parents were slain, she wanted to retreat from the world. She became isolated and depressed. Trevor forced her to push forward. He made her reengage with the world and gave her the confidence she needed to excel. It was only through his insistence that she played sports, and he attended every home game. He even made some away matches when his schedule allowed. His deep and endearing interest in her life got her through the malaise and helped to make her what she is today. While she was desperate to enlist his assistance, she also had to be careful that he didn't feel used. She owed him so much.

Chapter 10

Monday 7:00 AM, Waldorf Astoria Hotel, 1100 Pennsylvania Av., Washington, DC

Her third day on the run began in a similar fashion to the previous two. Only something was different today. She was calmer and filled with a sense of purpose. Was she starting to enjoy it, or was she just growing numb to danger? These questions need to be deferred to a later date. The task at hand needed her full focus and attention. She was keenly aware of what she needed to do, but how to contact Doctor Cameron Allen at the Smithsonian Institute was far from resolved. Mark and Cam were close friends, and Pamela had heard his name mentioned many times in conversation. The primary problem was that she had no idea of what he looked like.

A quick search on her laptop provided her with background information, but it took browsing several additional sites to obtain a photo. He was not quite what she expected. In his late thirties, Dr. Allen sported a sparse blonde beard and long hair slicked back. He looked more like Mathew McConaughey than Niels Bohr. More of an actor than a physicist. She learned he was also Director of the President's Council on Scientific Research. She equated this position with Mark's reference to power in his introduction. Access to the President of the United States was indeed power.

Her mind raced to formulate a plan. A bead of sweat made her aware that our Nation's Capital was considerably warmer than the Windy City. She opted to take a nice long shower. She always thought the best in there.

As the steaming hot water pelts her head, Pam's mind shuffles through a myriad of options. Email, text, and telephone all race through her head. But in a moment of clarity, she realizes something: this bazaar requires an equally odd encounter. She will literally bump into him and meet face to face. This was a bold plan, but circumstances dictated such action. She will stake out the lobby of his office building and wait for him to exit. Her first attempt will be at lunch, and if that fails, she will return at the day's end. Wrapped in luxurious towels, she exits the stall and sits on the bed. A quick glance at the clock gives her the time remaining to perfect her plan.

At the same moment, halfway across the country, Diane Vitullo sat in an aisle seat aboard a Boeing 737 on the runway at O'Hare International Airport. She was consumed with getting to DC as soon as possible and anxious to meet up with Lieutenant Detective Brad Jones of the District Police. A nervous flyer, Diane, fidgeted in her seat as the plane taxied for takeoff. She had to cut her conversation with Roger short when the plane suddenly jerked forward. Her partner was still sifting through leads from the credit card and license en route to General Mitchell Airport to see if any additional transactions appeared.

She wanted him to interview the flight crew of Pam's outbound flight to ascertain if she revealed any traces of her intentions or destination. It was a long shot, but most times, it's better than having no shot at all.

Diane spends the next two hours trying to overcome her flight anxiety until the wheels finally touch down and the jet comes to a stop on the tarmac. Relieved to be on solid ground, she exits the plane and is met at the gate by her young colleague.

Brad is eager for his first assignment working with the NSA. Recently promoted to detective, the 24-year-old was the product of humble origins. Born into a broken home in the heart of DC, he was raised by his young mother, who toiled laboriously to provide a stable home and a college education for her only son. Excelling in his schoolwork, he ultimately earned a bachelor's degree in accounting from the University of Virginia before entering the academy. He took nothing for granted. She was the proudest person on the planet the day her son graduated and became a law enforcement officer. This was only surpassed by the joy she expressed when he was handed his gold shield less than six months ago. The enthusiasm that dripped from his being was contagious and that is exactly what Diane needed as she walked through the gate and into the terminal.

After a brief introduction, Diane handed photographs of her target to Brad, who instantly distributed them to the two uniformed offers accompanying him. He instructed them to head directly to the cab stands and show the snapshots to as many people as possible. He motioned for Diane to follow him to the National Hall Starbucks, where he purchased two coffees and sat across a small table opposite her.

"Cream, one sugar… I did my research. So, what can you tell me to help me locate this woman? I'll also need to know her threat level."

Diane viewed her well-dressed companion and was impressed by his energy and the frankness of his inquiry.

"There are things I cannot reveal for security reasons, you understand that?" He nods. "But we are convinced she is a minimal threat risk, and we do not believe she is armed or violent."

"We would like you to issue an APB (All points bulletin) but keep it out of the press. All we need is a locate and we can take it from there."

Brad flashes his charming smile, "So you guys get all the glory?"

She returns the smile and promises to involve him as much as possible and give him all the credit he deserves.

They finish the coffee, and he looks at his watch.

"Let's go, we have video to watch. The airport director said we would be able to view it at 11:30 AM."

Knowing the arrival time of Pam's flight allowed the officers to focus on a one to two-hour time frame. They poured over several hours of video from different cameras without any positive identification. Their eyes became weary from watching passengers boarding, deboarding, or just sitting. There was simply no sign of the cute blonde in the photograph. Just when they were about to give up, Diane's cell phone rang, and she answered. Roger was on the line.

After interviewing the Milwaukee flight crew, one attendant noticed she was carrying a Brewers baseball cap and sunglasses.

Diane waves her hands, "Hold on, my partner has additional info."

He relays to Diane the eyewitness account that Pam had a Brewers cap and sunglasses with her on the flight.

"Bingo, I saw a female of similar stature wearing the exact same baseball cap at one of the gates. The big dark sunglasses covered her face. Rewind the video. I got her," she shouts, "I'm certain of it.

They pore over previously viewed tapes armed with new knowledge. It takes only twenty additional minutes for them to locate her.

Can we get a still? We need to be showing this to the cabbies and your patrol officers."

Brad speaks with Airport security, and by 3:00 PM, they have another item to distribute. They walk through the terminal, passing out copies of the new photograph, desperately seeking a breakthrough.

Diane informs Brad that she will be staying in town this evening and that she has dinner plans with family in Virginia. She exchanges cell numbers with him, asking to be informed if anything breaks. They shake hands, each making a fond first impression. The NSA agent heads toward the rental car counter, and her mind is now focused on the second phase of her trip.

She rents the car on a personal credit card, wanting to keep this portion of the trip concealed from official records. Within the hour, she is in a late model Ford sedan driving on the George Washington Parkway, looking for the Chain Bridge Road / Dolly Madison Boulevard Exit. On the trip, her mind wanders back to "Uncle Trevor's," walking into her bedroom as she lay sobbing on her pillow. His firm but gentle touch told her that everything was going to be OK. He always knew what to say or do to pick me up. Seeing him will bring back a ton of memories and emotions. She hoped she was prepared.

Adrift in memories, the ride passes quickly, and in a blink, she arrives at the Staybridge Suites on Old Dominion Drive. The hotel was strategically located just down the road from her 7:00 PM dinner reservation at J. Gilbert's Wood-Fired Steaks and Seafood. She hated asking for favors, but her instincts were telling her that this was necessary. Preoccupied with the upcoming meeting Diane does not notice the black SUV pulling into the parking lot behind her and two pairs of eyes intently watching her walk into the lobby and check in.

Her time at the front desk is minimized, wanting to allow enough time for preparation. She heads straight for her room, leaving nothing to chance. Everything must be perfect for the evening ahead. After a quick shower, she climbs into her finest suit. The navy-blue pinstripes compliment her hose and heels of the same color. Diane's dark hair is neatly brushed, and just the right amount of makeup is applied, followed by a dash of perfume. Elegant yet professional. At the age of twenty-seven, she still felt like a child in his presence. Her performance needed to be sincere but also purposeful. The feelings she harbored for the man who raised her must play second fiddle to the mission.

Chapter 11

Monday 4:30 PM, Lobby Smithsonian Institute Science Center, 600 Maryland Ave., Washington, DC

Pamela checked out of the Waldorf at 4:00 PM and walked along Pennsylvania Avenue to Seventh, where she turned south to continue the 18-minute walk to her destination. Arriving at Maryland Avenue, she made a left and stared at the large office building. Her heart was beating violently in her chest as she approached the entrance to the lobby, where she took a seat and waited while trying to look inconspicuous. Her decision to check out of the hotel was induced by the warning left behind by her fiancé and a desire to force herself into action. She had chickened out at lunchtime, watching him walk past with a couple of friends. She couldn't fall victim to her fear again.

The time to act was now. She stares at the analog clock on the wall, whose hands appear to stop moving. An attempt to swallow proves more difficult than expected. Her mouth was dry, but she was keenly aware of the dampness forming on her skin. After what felt like an eternity, she saw the elevator door's part and her target exit. He was alone. She has rehearsed this moment in her head for hours and as if someone yelled action on a movie set, she springs into motion. The plan was designed to be an "accidental" collision.

Their bodies bump on cue and her purse spills out onto the floor. They both lean down to pick up the contents. His blue eyes lock onto hers. An apologetic Cameron tries to assist by gathering up as many items as he can. As both their heads come together, she whispers into his ear.

"Doctor, I am Mark Stanton's fiancé. Can we talk in private?"

The puzzled researcher, still captivated by her angelic face and bright eyes, hears the name of his dear friend and nods in the affirmative.

"Can I buy you a drink?"

With no other options, she agrees, and he ushers her through the doorway and into the fall evening air.

They walk briskly down 7th Avenue when he turns and asks, "How is Mark?"

Noticing her immediate distress upon hearing the name, he ceases all conversation and pulls her across Blair Alley and into an establishment titled "Easy Company." The local wine bar/restaurant was a favorite along the DC waterfront. A twenty-dollar bill accompanies his request for a quiet table, which was a simple task to accomplish given the sparse Monday evening crowd.

The couple is seated, and he hands her a handkerchief to blot the now streaming tears. Feeling a bit inadequate, he asks, "How can I help you?"

"Mark disappeared and left me with these two flash drives. He wanted me to reach you. Please, I need you to look at the first one now. I have been going crazy since Saturday."

The waitress appears and they order two glasses of wine, one white and one red. He realizes this might take a while, so he requests menus.

She extracts her laptop from its satchel and opens it on the table. Inserting the flash drive, she lowers the volume so that only they can hear. The video begins as it did at the bank. The site of Mark causes another wave of tears as a befuddled Dr. Allen stares at the screen, mouth agape. Awestruck at the actions of his friend, he clings to every word. Alarm bells begin ringing in his head.

He tries to digest every nuance of the warning and questions why Mark instructed her to reach him. Somehow, he feels an obligation to his colleague and friend. One look at the fragile blonde sitting across from him settles any debate. They stop the video as the drinks are served, and Cam hands Pamela a menu. We better eat now and figure the rest out later.

They both order cheeseburgers accompanied by French fried potatoes and coleslaw. He tells her to relax, and they enjoy the meal without uttering another word. A second round of drinks is requested, and the waitress leaves after depositing the stemmed glasses on their table. Both try to cope with the awkwardness and the seriousness of their situation.

"OK, I have a plan. It's obvious Mark believes you're in danger, so you must stay with me at my place until I can sort through this. I'll need to review the other flash he sent to understand what caused his rebellion and why I was selected to remedy it."

With nowhere else to go, Pamela accepts the invitation, grateful not to be spending another night alone in a hotel room.

They each welcome the numbness that comes with the second drink. Cameron pays the check, and he takes his fragile companion by the arm. They make the two-minute walk to his Apartment on the second floor of the Channel Apartment Complex located on the wharf at 950 Main Ave. He tidies up the second bedroom where she will sleep tonight.

Trying desperately to soothe her, he stammers, "You'll be safe here. Get some sleep. We can talk in the morning."

Chapter 12

Monday 7:00 PM, J Gilberts Wood Fired Steaks and Seafood, 6930 Old Dominion Drive, McLean, VA

Diane is the first to arrive, and she is ushered to her uncle's private booth in the most secluded area of the restaurant. The waiter asks if she would like a drink, and she declines, wanting to be razor-sharp for this encounter. She hated asking for favors, but when the stakes were this high, she would do everything necessary.

Her cell buzzes, and noticing it is Brad, she answers. With no one around, his jubilant voice reverberates on the other end of the line. "We have a lead. The airport dispatcher claims one of his drivers picked up the woman in the cap. We can interview him tomorrow at the airport at 8:00 AM." "Brad, that's terrific! I'll see you there." Looking up, she notices Trevor at the entrance and rushes to end the call.

Her uncle was a tall, handsome man, always fit, tanned, and impeccably dressed. Coupled with his brimming confidence, he appeared a decade younger than his chronological age of 62. As he approaches the table, her body rises to hug the man who raised her as his own after her parents were callously murdered. She felt closer to him than anyone on the planet. His presence was comforting.

"I'm sorry I ran a bit late, but if you hadn't heard, I was nominated to take over the Directorship when Admiral Wilson succumbed to his heart attack last week. We are prepping for some tough Senate Hearings, but the odds are trending in my favor."

Diane, almost equal in stature in her heels, kisses him on the cheek.

"I am so happy for you uncle; I know how hard you have worked for this."

He ponders to himself; she will never know how hard.

Noticing Diane had not ordered a cocktail, he motions to the waiter, who nearly stumbles to reach the table promptly. Still looking at his "niece," he orders two dirty Tito martinis straight up with olives, waiting for some sign of approval. Her face lit up with a smile, and he knew the order was perfect. She sips her drink, marveling at the accomplishments of this man, born in the coal mines of West Virginia.

A football scholarship to Pitt and a stint in the Navy got him accepted into the FBI. He and my dad were classmates and then partners for fifteen years before he opted to become what we joked about, a spook. They remained close and he was the best man at my parents' wedding and soon thereafter became my godfather. They were happy times. Lost in the past, Diane realizes that her uncle is staring out at her.

She sips her martini a bit hesitantly. Sensing this, Trevor speaks, "It's alright, my dear Diane. I understand this is not purely a social call. Let it out. You do know I will do everything in my power, which is considerable, to help you."

Relieved by his offer, she responds, "As great as it is to see you, I do have an ulterior motive. I am so appreciative that you're not upset and willing to assist."

Her nerves settled, and the waiter was again summoned. "Shall we dine first and leave business for dessert?"

"I will have the New York strip medium rare with a baked potato and asparagus."

His companion opts for a filet of the same temperature, baked potato, and sauteed spinach. While the meal is being prepared, a bottle of Caymus cabernet arrives with two stemmed glasses. It is opened, tasted, and poured.

Before she can speak, the soon-to-be Director of the CIA praises her for her work at the NSA.

"I've been watching you rise through the ranks. You're an excellent detective, Diane. Your mom and dad would be proud of you. If you ever want to become a spook, I'll open the door."

They both giggle and she does thank him but informs him that she is quite happy where she is. Some light banter follows as the meal is served and devoured.

They sit across from each other, empty plates and a drained bottle between them. The dessert order consists of one espresso and one cappuccino. When the table is cleared, Uncle Trevor's face turns serious.

"Now, my lovely Diane, please let me know how I may assist you."

"I am working on a case which began at Fermi lab. A top scientist died, and I have been trying to get inside to do some interviews with his staff. There is so much we need to know, but we are getting stonewalled."

"Is this the suicide we heard about on Saturday?"

"We don't believe it is suicide. There is evidence that may point to murder. We are trying to locate his fiancé, who appears to be on the run. We know she is here in DC, but we don't know where."

Trevor raises an eyebrow, "In DC, you say?" His stoic face flinches ever so slightly. "So, who is stonewalling you?"

"An army Colonel by the name of Marshall Fielding, do you know him?"

"Not personally, but in my line of work, I have probably read something about him and most of the people residing within a 100-mile radius of this place. When do you fly back?"

"I land at O'Hare tomorrow afternoon around 6:00 PM Chicago time."

A chin rub elicited the following. "Be at Fermi at 10:00 AM on Wednesday. The Colonel will be expecting you."

Diane sat open-mouthed, barely able to get a single word out of her mouth. "How?"

The Deputy Director raises a finger to his mouth in a shushing motion, "We may not be allowed to act on American soil, but we are very close to those that can."

They both rise and exit the restaurant together, and his driver pulls up with a large black Lincoln while Diane fumbles for the valet ticket. An embrace and a kiss follow.

He whispers in her ear, "I may not have his job yet, but I already have his car."

She shakes her head, laughing and delighted by the outcome of this dinner both on a personal and a professional level. Weary, she is relieved that her hotel is right down the road, only minutes away.

Across Old Dominion Drive, the dash of a black SUV is illuminated by an outgoing cell call. Daniel Dryden is already in bed but answers when he sees the number.

"She dined with who?"

Now, trying to reign in his growing panic, he asks, "Are you sure?"

The voice of Jun Li never changes pitch.

"We know where she is staying, and we can eliminate her easily if that is your wish. Just give us the order."

"No, do nothing until I tell you."

A flustered CEO jumps from his comfortable bed and rushes across to his office, scrambling to enter the following message into his keyboard.

AGENT VITULLO HAD DINNER WITH TREVOR HAWTHORNE, DEPUTY DIRECTOR OF THE CIA, TONIGHT IN MCLEAN, VA. RIGHT DOWN THE STREET FROM OUR OFFICE. I HAVE AGENTS IN PLACE, AND WE CAN TAKE HER OUT TONIGHT.

Within seconds, a response is received.

NO ACTION IS WARRANTED AT THIS TIME. TO BE CLEAR, STAND DOWN UNTIL FURTHER NOTICE.

The trembling recipient searches madly in the top drawer for the jar of pills inside, nearly spilling the contents as he throws two tablets down his throat, washing them down with a half-filled water bottle. He mumbles to himself. "This makes no sense. She is getting too close and has too much access. What the hell is he thinking?"

Chapter 13

Tuesday 6:00 AM, The Channel Apartments, 950 Main Street, Washington, DC

Dr. Allen is sitting in front of his PC, marveling at the details downloaded onto the prized flash drive. His first duty is to make a copy and avoid risking the loss of this valuable information forever. He has been awake for over an hour, mesmerized by the ingenuity of his friends' experiments and what they have been able to accomplish.

His thought process was pure genius, and the protocol was a thing of beauty. The results were both astounding and frightening. Both he and Mark were always cognizant of their work being used for sinister purposes. Seems like the military loves to turn wonders into weapons. It takes someone of great intellect and instinct to devise procedures such as these. To see them used for destruction was heart-wrenching.

The Fermi team used enhanced high-energy harmonics to facilitate the Fractional Quantum Hall Effect, which transitioned three-dimensional material into two. Mark believed that sound was the ultimate energy, and when magnified properly, it could counter the strong nuclear force that binds all matter at the subatomic level. The objects disappeared for short windows, reappearing in minutes unaltered. The term "Blinking" was coined to describe this phenomenon.

Mark then complains of pressure from above to add more energy and expand the results. He cautioned against this. When more power was added, something remarkable occurred. The object vanished but in its place was something of equal mass never seen on this planet. Solid, pure energy. Something with wonderful potential but equally destructive. They named it the Pandora Particle.

When Mark noticed signs that the inventory was being toyed with, he used his experiment to catalog all the material produced. A Colonel was then put in charge and demanded more and more of the material for weaponization. That's when the anomaly appeared. A void. A gap in space. A pause. No one knew for certain what it was.

Mark knew he had to slow everything down. That's when he began sabotaging his own experiments. He realized that this was going to end badly without some drastic intervention. The algorithms he used remain only on this drive. All the files left at Fermi were deliberately corrupted. Panic ensued when he found out they were being monitored by an outside source, so he accelerated his plan and was forced to use the only remaining person he trusted to get this information to me.

Cameron sips on a large mug of piping hot black tea and rises, walking to the other end of the apartment to check on his guest. He opens the door just a crack to see her engulfed in a restful slumber. Probably her first night's sleep in several days. He closes the door, trying to get her lovely face out of his mind, and gets back to focusing on the larger issue at hand.

All his wile and clout would be needed to get this project back into civilian hands and somehow find a way to control the tear in space. He also must be sure to keep the information out of the hands of any bad actors. His final duty was to keep his friend's fiancé safe. She would be the prime target for someone wanting to get to his work. At the same time, he was dealing with the guilt of discovering he had feelings for the blonde doctor.

For the moment, she was safe in his apartment, but as he began to actively intercede at Fermi, things would change. Everything he had or owned would be subject to scrutiny. He had to find someone to trust. Someone who could harbor her during this process. All this thinking was making him hungry, so he entered the kitchen to prepare a hearty breakfast for two.

He opens the refrigerator and removes a carton of eggs, butter, and a packet of thick-cut bacon. Maybe I will think better on a full stomach. Tossing a fry pan on the stove he knifes off a chunk of butter and turns the dial. Just as he goes to crack the first egg, he gets an epiphany. "A shell." He turns off the stove and rushes back to the keyboard, reenergized. Can he develop an energy shell to contain the anomaly while they do further study? His hypothesis is that the physics of another reality intermingles with ours at that point. It rushed to fill the void when one of our dimensions was removed. A shell or barrier could contain any effects caused within it.

He starts to do some high-end math and thinks it is possible but realizes a more powerful computer is necessary to flush out the theory. This might be the solution needed. Just then, he notices those big blue eyes staring over his left shoulder.

"Up for a good breakfast?" he asks.

She grins a welcoming yes. The two enjoy eggs over easy, copious amounts of bacon and toast washed down with chilled orange juice. The leisurely pace is suddenly broken when he notices the time.

"Pam, I must go into the office this morning. Aside from keeping up appearances I need to check some calculations on the Institutes mainframe. It is important you remain here in the apartment. Do not leave or answer the door. Do you understand?"

She nods, not happy but accepting of the circumstances.

"I'll be back this afternoon, and we can work out a plan together. Your safety is the most important thing right now."

She responds with a thank you and an unexpected hug which lingers more than it should. Fetching his laptop and briefcase, Cam leaves the apartment for his fifteen-minute walk to the office, struggling to control his emotions and torn loyalties. Through the window she watches her only friend in the world hustle away. Left alone, she curls into a ball on the sofa, reacquainting herself with the feeling of isolation.

Chapter 14

Tuesday 9:00 AM, Ronald Reagan International Airport, Washington, DC

Detective Lieutenant Jones is pacing near the taxi stand at Ronald Reagen Airport, awaiting both the taxi driver and his NSA counterpart. Diane arrives first, carrying two large cups of coffee.

"You're not the only one who does research," she jests.

Brad smiles, and the two make small talk until the cabbie arrives nearly twenty minutes late. As a courtesy Diane allows the Detective to handle the interrogation, and he flashes his badge in the man's face. Ms. Wards' photo in the cap and sunglasses is shown.

"Yes, she was my fare on Sunday."

"We need you to check your records and tell us where you dropped her off," quips Jones, unable to conceal his excitement.

"No need, detective. I remember exactly where she got out. I took her to the Waldorf on Pennsylvania Avenue...I don't get many fares going there."

His inquisitors thank him and hand him a card should any more details come to mind. There is a moment of eye contact, and Brad yells, "I'll drive. I know the way." Diane climbs into the passenger seat, and they race off to the hotel.

The unmarked police car skids into the valet lane doors, flying open before coming to a complete stop. Badges are flashed. The door man and valet back away to the words, "Police Business." The front desk is located and they both rush to meet the clerk. She is a very professional middle-aged woman with an English accent. Badges still in hand she greets them unphased by the urgency of their approach. Knowing the alias used to purchase the plane ticket, Diane speaks first.

"Do you have a guest registered by the name of Vanessa Redfield? She would have checked in sometime Sunday afternoon."

The clerk responds, "Thank you for narrowing the time it does make it so much easier to locate. I'm sorry, officers. It appears that although she booked two nights, she checked out yesterday afternoon around 4:00 PM. The payment was in cash. Anything else I can do for you, officers?"

They thank the very efficient clerk and turn back toward the cars. With the photograph in hand, Agent Vitullo stops to chat with the doorman. "The woman left yesterday around 4:00 PM. Did you hail her a cab?"

"No, detective, we saw the pretty lady leave here on foot and walk east on Pennsylvania Avenue."

Another thank you is expressed, and they rush back to the hastily parked vehicle. A native of DC, Diane is familiar with the area. "She left on foot, so her end destination is somewhere close. Can you have your patrols concentrate within a twenty-block radius of the hotel? Make certain they have both photos."

Brad nods, "What next?"

"Let's cruise the area. I have some time to kill before my flight. We should work our way south from here to the wharf. We are close I can feel it."

The car pulls out and works its way east and south, looping about while she places a call to her partner in Chicago. When Roger answers Diane inquires if any additional charges were made on the credit card. He answers in the negative.

"I'm flying out on the 4:31 flight and will land in O'Hare at 5:44 tonight. We got the green light on a meeting at Fermi tomorrow at 10:00 AM. If you're open to it, I'd like to meet for dinner and discuss our plan of attack."

Roger eagerly accepts. "I can't wait to meet this, Colonel."

She makes another request. "Can you bring the list of scientists on the Fermi team? We might need to divide and conquer. We also traced Ms. Ward to the Waldorf on Pennsylvania Ave. We think she is close. Have our analyst compile a list of all Stanton's friends and associates with emphasis on anyone living in DC. Prioritize proximity to the Waldorf. We will handle Fermi tomorrow and be back here on Thursday. Thank you, Roger, you're the best."

"Where shall we meet for dinner, and you know you're buying," he chides.

They plan to meet at Dua's on Higgens Road at 6:30 PM. A ten-minute drive from the airport.

"Be careful, Diane. This case is starting to freak me out."

They end the call and focus on their immediate tasks at hand. After unsuccessfully scouring the neighborhood, they realize it's time to head back to the airport. Brad is happy to escort her, and she promises to notify him of any developments. A stroll through security delays matters a bit, but she eventually arrives at her gate. It's been a long day, and not knowing when it will end causes her to hope she can get some sleep on the plane ride home. Tomorrow will be a very important day with the added burden of making her uncle's favor count.

Outside security, the telephone number of ParTec Industries is dialed into a cellphone, and Kristen Dryden answers. The voice of Chen Zhao fills the speaker.

"The detective is at the airport flying back to Chicago. Do you want us to follow her back?"

Kristen advises that the private jet is fueled and ready to take them back to Chicago. "We are certain she will return to DC after the meeting, but we need you back here should anything unexpected arise. The Colonel has advised me she is meeting him at Fermi at 10:00 AM tomorrow. He must bow to pressure from above and take the interview, but she will learn nothing from him. I assume your surveillance will capture everything that transpires, and we can react accordingly. We will give the captain the order to take off when you reach the plane."

For the second time in successive nights, Diane arrives first for a dinner engagement. The plushness of the

Italian Restaurant was no match for the Virginia Steakhouse, but the food was good, and the location was convenient. She orders a glass of red wine and tries to figure out where Pamela is headed. Who or what would bring her to that part of DC? She had made absolutely zero progress when her partner strolled in carrying two big files.

"This is all Fermi," he says, "the analysts won't have anything until tomorrow morning."

"Fine," she replies, "let's eat first."

They both order the linguine and meatballs in a tasty Bolognese sauce. Roger goes with a beer. They finish eating and open the files, deciding who will interview who, but both want the Colonel together as a team. She hasn't met the man but already despises him. They continue working until closing time before departing for home. In the parking lot, Roger offers to pick her up for the ride to Batavia, and she graciously accepts.

Chapter 15

Tuesday 4:00 PM, The Channel Apartments, 950 Main Street, Washington, DC

Dr. Allen's day at the office was a hectic one. He ran multiple calculations and pored over research paper after research paper. Several theories were postulated, each to evaporate under closer scrutiny. His idea was sound, but he needed the correct method. He knew time was running short, and his frustration grew. Without having the luxury of experimentation, he knew the equations must be precise. It was nearly 2:00 PM when the eureka moment occurred. Everything clicked, and he downloaded the solution onto a flash drive. It seemed like everything of importance he encountered the past few days came from a flash drive. He cursed the inventor, shut down his laptop, and made his way out of the office.

On his way past, he advised his secretary that he would not be in tomorrow morning but would call for messages. He sets off for home. Cam returns to the apartment at 4:00 PM, having taken a bit longer than anticipated to formulate his plan. On his way back, he stopped at Ann's Beauty Supply and Wigs on L Street to purchase a brown wig. Portions of his plan are formulating in his brain. He is carrying a bag of groceries, and he tells Pam they will discuss their next moves over a gourmet dinner to be fashioned by none other than him. Before entering the kitchen, he places the wig, an old pair of sunglasses, and two track phones in a small travel bag with some other items.

The lighthearted nature of their conversation almost makes the circumstances pleasant. A bottle of Sauvignon Blanc is opened to make the prep time pass by without any complaints. He dons a white chef's hat to further lighten the mood wanting her in the best frame of mind possible. A large pot is placed on the range and filled with salted water for the main course, his famous fettuccine alfredo. He pulls out three different cheeses that work together as a team to become his secret Alfredo sauce. While the pot is heated to a boil, he prepares the appetizer. Having become a whiz with a knife, he dices the tomatoes and onion and tosses them into a bowl of olive oil and seasoning. The contents are spooned onto a crostini, and the bruschetta is placed on the table. He follows with a medium-sized Caesar salad.

Pam assists and sets the table so that he can work unfettered in the kitchen. She notices the presence of two candles on the table, and she lights them. The scene is quite romantic and more reminiscent of a date than a safe house. The first appetizer, a plate of bruschetta, is offered, and the two sit and munch while sipping their wine. Cam wants to get her in the right mood before revealing the plan he has conceived. Dinner is consumed, and a second bottle of wine is opened. The mood is almost giddy.

Pam gets lost in the moment, forgetting the circumstances that led to her being here. Seeing this, he hesitantly decides the time is right to reveal the next steps of his plan. Those he feels are needed to resolve the mess they are now both entangled in. After an awkward moment of silence, Cameron takes hold of Pamela's hand and gazes deeply into her eyes.

"What I am about to say is extremely important, and I need you to know that your safety is my primary concern. You understand that, don't you?"

"But I don't want to leave you. I feel safe here with you."

"When I surface with the flash drive, all eyes will be on me, both good and bad. This apartment will not be safe. The scrutiny of those meaning to stop us will be intense. The dangerous people that Mark warned you about will know to look here. I called my sister-in-law and made plans for you to stay with her for a couple of days until everything blows over. It's only temporary but it is necessary. Do you trust me?"

She nods.

"Ursula lives alone in a secluded single-family home in Chevy Chase. It is backed up to a park and is very private. She is a widow. My brother was a lawyer who never grew up. His career could never satisfy the restlessness inside him. He died two years ago in a boating accident. She has dealt with your pain and understands your loss. Her help will enable you to get through this. I have a plan in place, and I think it's a good one, but the less you know, the better."

A stunned Pamela stares up at him and makes only one request.

"Ok, but can I sleep in your bed tonight?"

He reaches out to embrace her tightly. He doesn't even know when the kissing began. Before long, they rip at each other's clothes. His shoes are kicked off, and he feels his shirt being torn from his body as he lifts the sweatshirt over Pamela's head, revealing her naked breasts.

Her blue eyes gaze at him. She is clearly in command, gently forcing him back into his bedroom. A part of him rebels in remembrance of his friend, but in this erotic dance, she is clearly leading. He falls back onto a king-sized mattress, unable to remember the last time it was used for anything but sleep. A night of torrid lovemaking ensues until both exhausted participants slip into a deep slumber.

Chapter 16
Wednesday 9:45 AM, Fermi Lab., Batavia, IL

The agents exit their vehicle and proceed to enter the Science Lab. They walk directly to the receptionist, surprised to find one dressed in the khaki uniform of a U.S. Army sergeant. They reach for their badges, and she tells them there is no need.

"We know who you are. Kindly have a seat over there. The Colonel will be right with you."

They sit for twenty-five minutes before the woman returns to usher them into the office of Colonel Marshall Fielding. Their plan was to have Diane serve as the interrogator and Roger the instigator, but the annoyance demanded a more aggressive approach. Sitting at his desk, the pompous officer does not even rise to greet them.

"Welcome, agents. I would like to keep this as brief as possible. My people are all assembled in the conference room, twirling their thumbs. I'd like to get them back to work as quickly as I can."

Diane responds, "It is not our intention to disrupt your work here, Colonel, but you do understand we have a job to do. The highest security cleared person in this lab is either missing or dead, and it is our responsibility to find out which and, if the latter, how."

With a stern voice, Fielding responds, "I also have a job to do, understand that."

The tone begins to get testy, and Roger interjects, "I see by your array that you served in combat, sir."

"I did, son, eight years, Desert Storm and Iraq II. The only true way to measure a man is in combat.

"That's true, sir, and it looks like you received a medal for the Fallujah campaign."

"Indeed, I commanded the support force when we took it back. One of my proudest accomplishments."

Diane pulls out a small recording device. "Sorry, Colonel, but these are much cheaper than stenos and don't worry, everything will be classified."

The arrogant man's face turns redder than a beet, but he remains calm. The transcript of the interview reads as follows:

DV: Thank you again. This is our interview with Colonel Marshall Fielding, Project Director of Fermi Lab, at 10:35 AM on Wednesday, September 25, 2024. Colonel, can you tell us if anything is missing from the lab?

MF: No.

DV: To clarify, is the no to signal that nothing was missing or that you can't tell us?

MF: Nothing was missing.

DV: Are you saying you are absolutely certain, sir? We have reason to believe Dr. Stanton removed something before he left.

MF: I said nothing was missing. Didn't you hear me? The traitor erased his own work files to sabotage a US military project. I don't care if he is dead or alive.

DV: Do you know of any reason why he would do such a thing?

MF: Who knows how these science geeks think? Most of them are weak, pathetic pacifists. Why do they do anything?

Roger nods to Diane and she pauses the tape.

"You know, Colonel, I fought in Iraq myself. Two tours eight years, Green Beret Bravo Company. I was in Fallujah fighting that day while we were waiting on your "resupply." Seems like you guys took the long way to get there to avoid potential enemy contact. We were almost out of ammunition. A lot of men died waiting for you. I agree; you can judge a man by his willingness to fight."

The Colonel's face is now ashen; he has lost the high ground.

Diane reengages the recorder.

DV: So, if this is a military project, why does the Pentagon disavow it?

MF: Well, it is, but it isn't.... you, you see, it possibly could provide some minor tactical advantages.

DV: And what might they be?

The man is melting like snow on an August sidewalk.

MF: That's classified.

DV: So, we have a disavowed project that's classified? Is that your answer, Colonel? Can't you understand why we are puzzled? Furthermore, its own inventor sabotaged the program and ultimately vanished.

MF: We don't know why he killed himself.

DV: Are you telling us he is dead, sir? Do you know something we don't?

MF: Well, I meant killed the project.

DV: Did he ever give you any reason as to why he would want the project dead?

MF: Like I said, these geeks are all pacifists.

DV: One last question, and we will move on. Did Doctor Stanton inform you that he was leaving?

MF: No.

DV: If that is the case, how can you be certain he didn't take anything? Did you watch him leave?

MF: Well, I mean, we didn't see anything …I mean, find anything gone. If you don't believe me, let's go talk to his people right now.

DV: This interview now terminates at 11:10 AM.

Diane clicks the recording device to the off position. She now looks across the table at a sweating, nervous shell of a man stripped of his pride and arrogance. "Oh, we intend to speak with them, but you can remain here. We prefer to do this our way."

Roger adds in one last insult, "Yes, sir and you seem to be comfortable watching the action from afar."

The pair rise and walk down the steps to the conference room. Midflight, Diane turns, "That felt so good." Roger snickers, "It did."

They enter the conference room, introducing themselves to the remaining staff. Diane asks if all personnel present worked while Mark was still here and all but two answer in the affirmative. She asks them to kindly wait in the lobby. One or both is a plant. "Before we begin, let us tell you what we know about the nature of your work here, and please, we ask you to point out any inaccuracies. Our primary duty here is to find out what happened to the man who led your team and what caused his change of heart."

Upstairs the Colonel is monitoring every word that is said. "We know you were using sound to try and affect matter in some way. Is that correct?"

Doctor Millstead raises her hand. "Yes, detective. We used enhanced harmonic resonance under high energy to break down the strong nuclear force binding all elements. However, people have been trying this for years. The concept is not new. It was Doctor Stanton's algorithms and his creative use of magnetic leveraging that created some success. He was very secretive regarding them, and one day, they were gone, erased from our system. He never returned."

"Do you know if he made any copies?" inquires Diane.

"If he did, detective, he didn't share with any of us."

The entire group responds to corroborate that statement.

Roger interjects, "Can anyone venture a guess as to what caused Dr. Stanton to question his own work? We are being told that it was because of its military implications."

This question causes considerable unease in the room...eyes turn away, unwilling to make direct contact with the questioner. The agents recognize the distress and realize the room is being monitored. No one wants to respond for fear of losing their jobs or more severe penalties.

Diane shifts the conversation. "OK, when was the Doctor last seen, and by who?

A man waves from the back. "I work the night shift. He was here until at least 10:30 Friday evening. I saw him at his desk. He looked a bit preoccupied."

"Are there any other people of his equal in the field? Someone we could contact to get more familiar with the science involved."

Dr. Millstead responds, "I can prepare you a list before you leave but he was by far ahead of the field."

"Thank you, Doctor. We will stop by to pick up the list after we notify the Colonel that we are finished."

The duo walks back up the stairs and knocks on the office door. "Come in," grunts Fielding, some confidence regained from hearing that his intimidation of the staff has succeeded in preventing any leaking.

"I could have saved you a lot of time and effort, agents."

Roger retorts, leaning into the man, "But then we wouldn't have had the pleasure."

They walk back down the steps, and Diane passes Dr. Millstead's cubicle. She is handed the list and given a very odd look. The second in command grips her hand tightly when passing the notepaper as if to signal something. Diane thanks the Doctor for her assistance and starts to fold the paper and place it in her briefcase when she hears a billowing voice from up above.

"Agent Vitullo," the Colonel shouts, "We need to see everything that leaves the facility. We can't risk giving up any secrets."

The Sergeant receptionist appears, holster unlatched, and in a rough and curt manner, rips Diane's case from her hand, opens it, and hands the paper to the smug Colonel. The tension in the room rises to a crisis level. Dr. Millstead slumps in her desk, and her breathing halts as the man in charge peruses the "list." After several agonizing seconds, he refolds the note and hands it back to the Sergeant. She returns it to the briefcase and hands it to its owner. Diane reaches for the strap of her case, glaring into the eyes of its bearer.

"I hope we meet again, Sergeant Kelly, is it?"

She and Roger turn and head for the car, still a bit puzzled. When they get inside, she looks at the list and smiles. Her partner asks her to see it and disappointedly states that there is nothing their analysts couldn't provide. Diane smiles, "Just drive to the nearest diner."

"By the way, where did you get the idea to use the recorder? I thought he was going to stroke out right there."

Diane smiles, "Oh, I just wanted to twist his gonads for making us go through hoops to get the interview. He is such a pompous ass. Did you see his face? Any bit of joy I can pull out of this case is worth it."

Roger knows just where to go and turns south on Kirk toward Butterfield. Destination: the Honey Milk Restaurant on Rt. 59 in Warrenville. He turns left on Butterfield and makes another left on Rt 59, arriving seventeen minutes after the request. They walk in and take a booth. Diane smiles. Read this one more time.

The list was simple:

1.) Dr. Cameron Allen..Smithsonian Institute (xxx) xxx-xxxx

2.) Dr. Sheila Pederson...UC Santa Clara (xxx) xxx-xxxx

3.) Dr. Emile Toureault...CERN (xxx) xxx-xxxx

4.) Dr. Rita Tartaglia...MIT (xxx) xxx-xxxx

5.) Dr. Pandora Hesiod…University of Athens (xxx) xxx-xxxx

Rogers stares and again shows his lack of enthusiasm for the document.

"I guess you never attended any classes on Greek Mythology," jokes his partner. "Pandora is the woman who opened the box, letting all the evils out into the world. The story was written by the Greek poet Hesiod. This is a clue. Dr. Millstead wants to warn us, and she wants us to call this number."

They order when the waitress arrives, and upon her leaving, the phone is hastily dialed.

It rings six times then a message begins to play. "If you dialed this number, then my clue was successful. They have indeed unleashed Pandora's curse. Dr. Stanton's experiments created a tear in space. We are still not certain of what it is or how it came to be. We fear it is growing in power and has the capability of destroying everything. The military wants to use it to create weapons, but they cannot control it. There is the potential for great danger. I live on a cul-de-sac on Mayfair Court in Warrenville, IL, meet me there at 7:00 PM this evening. I have more proof I can offer you. You must stop them. I will wipe this message after it is heard, and you will be able to text me at this number to confirm receipt."

They look at the address, and Roger remarks that it's less than five minutes from here. We should scout the area first, then head back to HQ to prepare. On the ride back, they discuss whether to inform their supervisor of Professor

Millstead's note. They decided against it fearing that the powers to me might expose her, and she could face serious professional consequences from the fallout. Both agents are very protective of sources. Upon arriving back at the office Roger looks down at his desk to see the analysts' report he had ordered. He waves the file over his head, and Diane, already out of her shoes, comes running over barefoot to get a glimpse. He yells, "Bingo," it looks as though one name appears prominently on both lists, and that person works at the Smithsonian and lives in DC.

Diane voices, "He's our guy, I know it."

"We got work addresses, a bio, a home address, and some good photos. It's all here. I'll make a copy for you and book our flights for first thing in the morning." Finally, they are making some progress. They got into Fermi and have learned a lot, with more to come tonight. The noose is tightening around the elusive Pamela Ward. Playing into the Greek Mythology theme Diane texts, Prometheus will arrive at the appointed time.

"I feel there is still something not right about this case." says a penseful Diane. "Did you notice that the Colonel seemed to know that Stanton was dead? If he did, who informed him?

"I got that," replies Roger. "I told you this whole bazaar scenario is freaking me out. Something stinks."

Roger looks at his phone. "Hey, they just found Ward's car. It was parked at a hotel down the road from the airport. She took a shuttle to the airport. This girl must be watching too many Jason Bourne movies."

Diane cautions, "Let's peel one layer at a time, partner. That's all we can do. But I do agree. I get the feeling we are only seeing the proverbial tip of the iceberg. Get me the file copy. I'm going to do some research on our date tonight."

Chapter 17

Wednesday 3:00 PM, Penthouse ParTec Industries, Old Dominion Drive & Lowell Ave, McLean, VA

Daniel Dryden complains to his sister about the NSA agent dining with the CIA. "We should eliminate that bitch now," he growls. "I can't understand why ICE is holding us back."

"Relax, Daniel, the man knows what he is doing. He has made our family a lot of money over the years. I cannot remember him ever being wrong. We owe our business to him."

"But this time he is, I can feel it."

They both fidget in their seats, waiting for the screen to energize. When it does, the large head of Colonel Fielding appears in close view. Dryden attempts to start cordially, "Colonel, it is good to see you. Please tell us how the NSA meeting went this morning."

The military man's brash persona is restored, and he responds, "It went like I told you it would. Those slide-rule jockeys didn't have the spine to resist my intimidation. I monitored the meeting on a closed-circuit video. Most of those geeks were afraid to even look up, let alone speak. No one said a peep."

Dryden tries to get more information, "Colonel, are you certain?"

He is met with a gruff reply. "Didn't you hear me? I am damn certain."

Realizing the man's bravado could not accept anything but praise, Kristen interjects, "We are glad you feel so strongly, Colonel. Thank you for the report." She terminates the video feed.

Daniel turns, "What did you do that for? We need to find out what happened."

"That's true, my brother, but don't you think we have better sources?" Kristen begins to contact their two mercenaries and soon they appear on the screen.

This time, they are both seated in the same room. Not much has changed in their appearance. Chen Zhao speaks first. We are happy to report that nothing was disclosed by the staff. We do believe that Colonel Fielding slipped and provided some clues, but we are confident nothing escaped that is critical right now. He is a problem that will need to be addressed in the future. Daniel exhales and begins to speak when he is cut off by Jun Li.

"My partner is correct, but I believe Dr. Millstead is planning to betray us. She was asked to provide a list of names, and it is my opinion she used that as an opportunity to arrange a meeting with NSA agents."

A tense Dryden asks, "Are you sure?"

Jun Li coldly responds. "Yes, she needs to be expunged. Sooner or later, she will talk."

"OK, thank you both. We will get back to you shortly using the normal channels."

Daniel walks to the bar, his hands shaking, and he pours two drinks. The first a bourbon on the rocks for him the second a gin and tonic for his sister. They have a nervous fifteen minutes to kill, and Kristen spends the time calming her brother down. At precisely 4:00 PM, the screen lights up again. On it, these words appear:

TELL ME WHAT OCCURRED AT FERMI TODAY.

A perspiring CEO responds by typing the following into his keyboard:

THE COLONEL FEELS EVERYTHING WENT WELL BUT HE IS A BUFFOON. MY OPERATIVES VIEWED EVERYTHING INDEPENDENTLY. WE BELIEVE WE ARE IN DANGER OF A LEAK FROM STANTON'S NUMBER TWO. THEY NOTICED A SUBTLE INTERACTION WITH THE AGENTS, AND THEY HAVE ASKED FOR PERMISSION TO ERADICATE.

I KNOW THAT MARSHALL IS AN IDIOT, AND WE WILL DEAL WITH THAT DOWN THE ROAD, BUT ARE YOUR AGENTS CERTAIN THAT PROFESSOR MILLSTEAD IS GOING TO TALK BASED ON A SUBTLE INTERACTION?

Daniel, sweating more now, responds:

THESE TWO ARE TRAINED AND HAVE GREAT INSTINCTS. IF THEY BELIEVE IT, SO DO I.

I AM NOT GOING TO ORDER MURDER BASED ON THE INSTINCTS OF FOREIGN MERCENARIES. YOU HAVE PERMISSION BUT ONLY IF THEY ARE CONVINCED. DO YOU UNDERSTAND? IF THEY ACT WITHOUT BEING CERTAIN, I WILL MAKE THEM PAY.

The armpits of Dryden's shirt are darkened with moisture. His stress is blatantly evident. He is quite happy that the entity known only as ICE cannot witness his current condition. Always obedient, he types:

IT IS UNDERSTOOD. I WILL GIVE THE ORDER AS SPECIFIED.

The communication is terminated, and Kristen hands him another bourbon as he begins to order the death of another human being under the terms dictated. He downs the drink in one gulp and gazes at his sister, wondering how she can be so calm.

Chapter 18

Wednesday 6:00 PM, Mayfair Ct., Warrenville, IL

The Cadillac turns onto Mayfair Ct. and slowly rolls past the trim split level they identified as the home of Dr. Stephanie Millstead. They drive past, u-turning three hundred yards beyond the residence and stopping on the opposite side of the street, approximately half that distance from the entrance. The lights and engine are turned off, and the agents slink back, waiting for the owner to arrive.

At Fermi, Dr. Millstead is ending her shift and nervously walks to her locker to exchange her lab coat for a light windbreaker. Slight in stature, she must rise to her toes to reach for her car keys on the top shelf. The echo of her racing heartbeat feels like the pounding of a drum. Her mouth is dry, and she feels overheated. Her smock-like dress and white tights now absorb the sweat from her body. She keeps glancing left and right, overwhelmed by the sensation of prying eyes. This is not a good feeling. Her murmured heart must be stressed, and she can't wait for the suspense to end. With any luck, in an hour, it will. The walk to her Prius parked in the garage seems to last an eternity. She gazes at the empty spot to her left. The sign: Reserved Dr. Mark Stanton, Project Director, still adorns the front wall. She pauses for a moment to mourn her lost comrade. The key fob falls to the floor as her hands are moist and nearly useless, but she perseveres and retrieves it. She opens the door and slowly bends into the front seat, gazing into the rearview mirror every thirty seconds. The engine starts almost silently, and the Professor begins her journey home.

The Prius begins to follow the same path as the white Toyota of her mentor, and she turns right onto Kirk Rd. She heads south, knowing the seven-minute ride will be over soon. At Butterfield Rd., she turns left toward IL Route 59 and her last leg home. The Asian mercenaries follow discreetly behind her when her car turns left on Rt. 59 Jun Li places the fake strobe light on the top of the roof and tells Chen to pull her over. "It's time." Chen looks puzzled. "Shut up and do as I say." quips his partner. They catch up to their prey at the entrance to the Honey Milk Restaurant, and the ever-law-abiding scientist pulls into the parking lot, wondering what traffic law she has violated. She rolls down her window and turns, expecting to see a law enforcement officer. The vision of Jun Li looking down at her will be her last. A thumb thrust into her throat is all it takes to end her life. The door was opened, and the body whisked quickly into the SUV. In seconds, the assassins speed away mission accomplished. A nervous Chen questions her action. "What are you doing? We were told to be certain before we acted." Jun Li held up her phone. On it, a map is displayed with a blue dot showing the location of Agent Vitullo's stationery just yards from the small split-level Stephanie called home. "Are you certain now?" an irritated Jun Li questions. "Remember the tracking device I placed in Tall bitches holster?" Both wore smiles and took joy in killing, and it had been too long since their last.

From their perch in the Cadillac, the agents wait patiently. 7:00 PM passes without any sign of activity.

Vitullo and Edwards become restless, barely able to wait until 7:45 PM. Diane redials their cell number, and it goes into voicemail. She dares not leave another message. At that point, with nothing to lose, she asks her partner to creep up several feet and remain in the car as a lookout while she searches the vacant house. Using her flashlight and her skills she quickly picks the entry lock. *Modestly furnished, she fumbles about the entrance with her torch until she notices* the drapes are drawn. Only then does she turn on a small lamp. Able to see, she locates and searches the Doctors desk and laptop. She finds a couple of files briefly referencing the anomaly and looks at several photos in awe. Some are digital inside the computer, and others are lying on the desk. The E-files are downloaded into a flash drive with Diane fidgeting every second. The hard copies were placed in her pocket. She is by no means skilled in physics, but what she sees and reads blows her mind. Her instincts scream at her to erase all the evidence on the PC, but she doesn't. She further delves into the mysterious particle, and the implications shock her. She now understands why Doctor Stanton sabotaged the work. She then focuses on the mysterious anomaly. It became clear to her that no one, not even the geniuses on site, knew what they were dealing with. There was no way the Colonel could comprehend any unintended consequences more tampering with the universe could do.

Meanwhile, Roger begins to place a trace on the cell phone, and by the time Diane exits with what she hopes is a clue, the location is triangulated.

"I got her phone it's only minutes away." Shouts Roger.

"Maybe she got cold feet," responds Diane over the noise of screeching tires.

The SUV speeds to the scene in less than five minutes making an abrupt turn into the nearly vacant parking lot of the Honey Milk Restaurant where they ate only hours earlier. They look up to see a light green Prius haphazardly parked across two spaces. Drawing their weapons the agents carefully leave their automobile and proceed forward with extreme caution. Roger covers Diane while she carefully opens the driver's door to avoid disturbing any evidence. She instantly sees the cell phone lying under the front mat and curses. "They got her, Roger." He quickly looked inside the restaurant to be confident she wasn't inside. When confirmed he responds, "I'll call it in." In fifteen minutes, NSA agents combined with local police swarm both locations, preserving them as crime scenes. Forensic units arrive and scour both properties for any vestiges of a clue.

Diane sits in the Cadillac in silence. Her tear-filled eyes gaze out and the flashing lights and frenetic activity. She knows the murderers tracked them. They are the reason Dr. Millstead is missing and, more than likely, dead. She was careless, and someone paid the price for it. An oath is taken right there in the front seat. Diane vows to catch the villains that did this. Killing her at the Honey Milk Restaurant was a signal. They were rubbing the agent's noses in it. The battle was lost, but Diane swore that they would win the war.

Roger and Diane exit the car and converse with several agents at the scene. When they are convinced both places have been secured, they return to their vehicle, aware that they have an early flight in the morning. Seeing Rogers packed bag in the back seat Diane asks if he would like to stay at her place tonight. He agrees. The two have really bonded, not only as partners but as friends. She respects the rock of a man sitting beside her, and he reciprocates. The tall woman has overcome any initial resentment that may have accompanied his reporting to someone of her age. They return to the Mode, and Diane shows Roger the spare bedroom.

"Im going to heat up a tray of lasagna. Can I pour you a glass of wine, or are you sticking with beer?" she teases.

He answers cleverly, "If we are going to be partners, I guess I better get accustomed to the grape."

During dinner, they reviewed some of the items in the file and the photos of the object Dr. Millstead referred to as the "anomaly." Their next step is clear. They need to reach Dr. Cameron Allen and learn what this thing really is. She pauses to give Detective Jones a courtesy call, and he graciously agrees to meet them at the airport in the morning. After devouring the hot meal and fine wine, the agents retire to their respective bedrooms, hoping to get some real sleep.

Chapter 19

Thursday 7:00 AM, The Channel Apartments, 950 Main Street, Washington, DC

Each awakens the next morning, not certain if last night was real or a dream. There is little conversation while both take a shower and dress. Dr. Allen finds himself in the most unusual of circumstances. He is handsome but not one with a busy social calendar. Last night was a rare occurrence in his life. He fumbles awkwardly to try and restore some normalcy between them. Pamela looks up once more, her blue eyes so enticing, and she breaks the silence. He may be her superior in intellect, but she is clearly more experienced in matters of the heart. They embrace for a kiss that seems to last decades. This was becoming personal.

"Thank you, Cameron," she says softly, "last night was wonderful."

His stupor is broken when he looks at his watch. He hurriedly tells her to remember to take all her things.

"You must not leave any clues behind."

They walk off to the garage holding hands and enter his Volvo sedan. In it, they exit the building together to begin the twenty-two-mile trek to Chevy Chase. It seems like hours before the vehicle pulls off I-385 and onto Connecticut Avenue. She clutches his wrist, squeezing tightly, knowing the destination is near. She does not want to let go. A turn onto Jones Bridge Rd. and another finds them in the driveway at the end of Hawkins Lane, a four-bedroom ranch house and possibly her sanctuary.

Pamela cannot quickly locate her baseball cap, so she ducks her face into Cameron's shoulder on the walk to the front door. She hears the doorbell ring.

Ursula Allen nee Sandstrom answers the door dressed in a tee shirt and jeans. After two years she has gone back to using her maiden name. The similarity of the two is remarkable and does not go unnoticed by all parties. Cam says, "Sis, this is Pamela, the woman I spoke to you about. We both thank you for helping and allowing her to stay here a couple of days."

"Don't be ridiculous, Cam. I am always here to help you and your friends. I, more than anyone, know what she is dealing with." She turns to Pam, "My brother-in-law may be a genius in some things, but he's an idiot in many others. Come on in, dear, and make yourself at home. Would you like a cup of tea? I will do my best not to bore you during your stay." Cam states that he would like to have a cup but needs to get back to attend to important matters. He hands Pamela's small bag to his sister-in-law and turns to leave.

Walking to the car, he hears, "Is this all you own, dear? Don't worry. It looks like we are the same size." A brief smile creases his mouth until he realizes how crucial the next twenty-four hours will be. The Volvo heads to Vienna, VA where it slides into a parking spot in front of the Extended Stay America Motel on Old Courthouse Road. The brown wig is affixed to his head, and along with an old pair of sunglasses, his image is altered just enough to match one of the fake licenses Mark left behind.

He enters the lobby and uses the matching credit card to book a two-month stay. Once in the room he sets up his laptop to finish altering one of the flash drive copies just enough to ensure it will not work without his presence. He also adds his containment solution disguised in an algorithm. One final quick overview to be sure. He then uses a roll of duct tape to secure the original flash drive to the bottom of the hotel desk.

Sitting on the bed, he notices his rapid breathing and some dampness in his clothing. He adjusts the thermostat to lower the temperature, trying in vain to calm his nerves. The next few hours will be critical for him, Pam, and possibly the whole world. He pulls out one of the trac phones and dials the number for Barry Armstrong, Chief of Staff, President of the United States. As head of the President's Council on Science and Special Projects, Cameron has some clout within the White House. Barry accepts the call and opens with, "Cameron, how the heck are you doing? Sorry I missed you at the last luncheon. I was called out of town."

"No worries, Barry. We will catch up later. Is he available? I have a matter of grave importance I need to discuss."

"Sorry, old friend, he left on Air Force 1 this morning heading for Wisconsin and Minnesota. It seems there is a small concern about these swing states brewing within the campaign. With the election only months away, our man wants to take no chances. You know he never misses an opportunity to get that mug on TV. He won't be back until Monday and wants to milk the weekend airtime."

"Damn, Barry, I have a matter of utmost concern regarding Fermi Lab. I don't think it can wait until then. Can you reach out to him?"

"Sorry, Cam, the campaign boys are in charge now through November. I would need a whole lot of facts to even get his attention."

"Ok, do you think you can put me in touch with someone else then? It is a high-security matter with bona-fide danger to it. I'll need someone of a high level."

"OK, old pal, let me make some calls, but are you certain you want to get involved in this?"

"I don't have a choice."

"OK, I'll see who has jurisdiction over Fermi and something like this. Don't stress, my friend. I am certain someone will step up. I'll call you back."

"Thanks for your help but I will call you back in an hour, ok?"

"Whatever works, Cam, whatever works."

The call terminates and Cam is left to pace the hotel room for the following sixty minutes. This new twist is unexpected but something he hopes he can navigate around. He stares at his face in the mirror wondering whether he has the guts to go through with this. But then his mind drifts back to last night and his affection for the woman he has vowed to protect. He will do everything in his power to make certain she remains okay.

Chapter 20

Thursday 9:00 AM, Ronald Reagan International Airport, Washington, DC

Detective Brad Jones waits patiently at the gate, having used his badge to circumvent security. The flight to DC is due to arrive in twenty minutes. He realizes that he has time to race to Starbucks and purchase two coffees, seeking to impress the beautiful female detective. The line is quite long, and he returns to the gate just as the passengers are disembarking. Diane's tall frame is instantly noticed. The thick man striding beside her blends in until they are face to face. He offers one coffee outward to Diane, and she smiles.

Roger looks at Brad and utters, "That must be mine, cupcake." With that, he whisks the cup from a startled Brad's hands, leaving his mouth slightly ajar.

He hears her voice saying, "Oh, Brad, let me introduce you to my partner, Agent Roger Edwards. Roger, this is Lieutenant Brad Jones, DC Police. He's the impressive young man I have been telling you about."

Doing his best to restore his composure, the young man extends his hand. The resulting grip and handshake nearly brought him to tears.

Taking a moment to recover, he inquires, "How may I be of assistance, agents?"

A tablet is removed from her briefcase, and photographs are shared. "This man works at the Smithsonian Institute. Can you get us there quickly?"

"No problem," is the immediate response. "That's assuming I can still grip the steering wheel." everyone chuckles as they rush to the car with the young man still painfully flexing his hand.

At that moment, unseen by the trio inside the terminal, the landing gears of a Gulfstream G-650 titled to ParTec Industries touch the earth, breaking to a sudden stop. The doors open, and two figures emerge from the fuselage, navigate down the stairs, and enter a black SUV parked for their arrival. Once inside the female opens her cell phone to relocate the signal she has been tracking. She never needed a reason to kill, but it was always more pleasurable when she disliked the victim.

The unsuspecting agents walk through the terminal and deploy into Lt. Jones's unmarked cruiser. Their destination was the Smithsonian. The car speeds across the Long Bridge, which crosses the Potomac River parallel to the Interstate and arrives on Maryland Avenue within eight minutes.

Using their status to minimize any security delays, they rush into the lobby. Brad heads straight for the reception desk while Vitullo and Edwards search the directory. Together they collaborated to learn his office is on the top floor of the east wing. It appears to be an addition looking somewhat newer than the remainder of the structure. In seconds the three are holding their breath inside a cramped elevator heading upward. The target they seek could provide the answers to the multiple questions posed.

Hope fades into heartbreak when his secretary advises that Dr. Allen has already called in to advise he will not be in the office today. Trying to mask their disappointment, Diane requests that she inform her boss of the importance of their quest. They need to speak with him as soon as possible.

"Would it be possible for you to call him on his cell phone for us?"

The secretary's attempt goes right into voice mail, but sensing the urgency, she responds with, "He did say he would be calling in later."

"Thank you, Tracey. Would you please give him my card? It is a matter of vital importance. I cannot stress that enough." Dianes' eyes meet with hers, and she tries her best to reinforce the seriousness in a nonverbal manner. Message received. Tracey promises to do her best to accommodate their request.

"Where to now?" asks Detective Jones.

"His residence," replies Roger.

As the team makes its way to the car, Brad inquires why they didn't request his telephone number. Diane and Roger look at each other, grinning. "We got that from her dialing. Remember, it's all in the details, Brad."

The name of the apartment building and its address are uploaded, and all realize the building is only minutes away. The car makes its way down 7th Avenue towards the wharf. A moment later, the trailing black SUV inches out of its perch and follows at a safe distance.

When they reach Maine Ave., they turn quickly and pull into the Channel Apartments garage. Noticing the Doctor's parking space is vacant, they drive directly into it. Six legs rush to the second floor using the stairs, and they nervously ring the doorbell, resisting the urge to break and enter. After three rings and two furious knocks from Edward's massive fist, Diane knows what she must do.

But first, she turns to the Lieutenant and whispers, "You better take a walk." He begins to protest, and she responds, "You're local, and you don't want to be here for what we do next."

He gets the message and goes to wait in the car. Roger may have strong hands, but they can also be delicate. He deftly picks the lock and has the front door open in seconds. With sidearms at the ready, they skulk into the apartment. The living room area is scanned first and reveals nothing. Moving into the dining area, Roger notices two candles and two unfolded napkins still on the table. In the kitchen, Diane opens the dishwasher and finds two of the following: plates, forks, and spoons. She also sees a pair of wine glasses, one with a red smear at the rim.

"She was here, Roger; I can feel it." He nods, knowing to trust his partner's instincts. When they enter the main bedroom, more evidence mounts. The large bed is ruffled, and both pillows have been slept on. Final confirmation comes when they reach the second bedroom, and a Milwaukee Brewers cap protrudes from the bottom of the bed. The exuberant agents exchange a high five. "That's it. He's our guy. Let's wait downstairs a bit while we check out if he has any relatives in the area. He might return."

They find Jones in the car and ask if he can request a stakeout of the location to make certain no one else enters the apartment. He agrees and offers to buy his colleagues' lunch at the Bistro Du Jour just down the street so they can keep an eye on the garage until the stakeout team arrives.

All are hoping they get the call, but they need to formulate an alternative strategy in case it never comes. While the agents dine in the air-conditioned restaurant, a dark SUV bakes on the street in the afternoon sun. Diane notices the vehicle and it seems to be a bit all too familiar.

"Roger, that's the same SUV that has been lurking about since we got here. I think I recognize the plate."

"It's impossible for them to have been following us. Something is wrong."

Brad speaks up. "Let me have an officer drive past the car so we can identify who is inside."

Both agents chime in, "Great idea."

Chapter 21

Thursday 12:00 PM, Extended Stay America Hotel, 8201 Old Courthouse Rd., Vienna, VA

A tense Cameron Allen uses one of the track phones to call Barry Armstrong back as promised. He needed to see if his associate was able to make any progress in finding him a contact within the government with sufficient clout to engage in this matter.

"Listen, Pal, you owe me. I pulled out all the stops for you within the intelligence community. This better be good. I don't like eggs on my face."

"No, Barry, I can assure you this is serious. I so wish it weren't."

"OK, Cam, listen carefully. I was instructed to have you dial the following number. When answered, you must order a **bourbon on the rocks**."

"Is this a joke?"

"No, my friend, it's no joke. These are serious people. You wanted access I got it for you. Now, do what they say. I pray for both our sakes that you're not batshit crazy."

Cam once again paces the room, unsure of what he's getting himself into. The confidence he had in his plan moments ago is waning under the pressure of the moment. He wants to speak to Pam one last time and he dials his sister-in-law's number. She answers and hands the phone to her border. The tone of their conversation reveals much more than the dialogue, and Ursula begins to understand how close the two have become. He manages a painful goodbye, knowing he must get about his business.

There is one more task to perform before THE call is made. The office schedule needs to be settled in the event he is missing for an extended period. A call is placed to his secretary, and he informs her of a pending issue and his potential absence. Having spoken to the NSA agents earlier, her concern is elevated. She relays the details of the meeting and asks if everything is all right. Cam shrugs it off as Tracey forwards Diane's cell number to him directly from her card. "I like her. I think you should call." Always gracious, Cam thanks her for the advice and disconnects.

Some unidentified urge pushes him to dial Agent Vitullo's number. She answers and nearly spits her Caesar salad onto the small table at Bistro Du Jour when he identifies himself. After regaining her composure, Diane responds, "Dr. Allen, thank you so much for calling. I am here with Agent Edwards, and we are investigating the death of your friend and colleague, Dr. Mark Stanton. We can confirm to you he has indeed died in a tragic automobile accident, but the circumstances surrounding it are quite puzzling. Please hear me out. We know that he sabotaged his own experiment and smuggled something out of the lab. We are quite confident he sent the material to his fiancé and that there is at least one nefarious entity looking for it and her as well. We also know that she flew to DC and stayed in your apartment last night. Listen to me. You are both in grave danger. Let us help you. Let us protect you."

"You are correct, Agent Vitullo, is it? However, there is a lot more going on, and I am the only one who can fix it. Mark was a good man, and he did what he did for the good of his country and the good of the planet. I must finish this for him. I cannot trust anyone else, including yourself. I must do this my way."

"You don't understand, Cam. We have been to Fermi and interviewed Colonel Fielding. There's something rotten there. They don't want to fix anything. They want his work and, in my opinion, will stop at nothing to get it."

"I am counting on that Agent; I have a plan, and only I can execute it."

"They will kill you, Doctor Allen. You must listen to me. Let us help you."

"I am very sorry, Agent Vitullo, and I believe you, but I know what I am doing, and I must do it my way. The consequences are too great."

The call disconnects, and Diane utters a shrill curse that turns every head in the restaurant in her direction.

Without hesitation, Cam dials the number he was given, knowing that any delay could result in his abandoning the plot. A voice answers, "Thank you for calling the COME IN AGAIN LOUNGE. How may we serve you today?"

"I'd like to order a bourbon on the rocks, please." He can't believe he is uttering these words that sound as if they belong in a Cold War B movie.

"One moment, sir, I will forward you to the proper department. Please hang on the line."

After several tense moments, he hears a familiar voice. Well educated with a slight southern drawl.

"Hello, Dr. Allen. I trust you remember my voice."

"Yes, sir, I believe we have met in the White House on at least one occasion, and I just saw you on TV with Senator Cosgrove."

"It is so kind of you to remember. You are correct. Your presentation on the practicality of designing a workable tractor beam device was very enlightening and quite impressive."

"Thank you very much, sir. I appreciate it."

"So, Cameron, if I may, I am sure now, knowing my involvement, you agree that we are taking this matter with the seriousness it deserves. Some bad actors are involved, and I am concerned for your safety. Do you have the information everyone is looking for?"

"I do, sir."

"OK. Here's the plan. We need to bring you in and get you in a safe house for your own protection. We can debrief you there. Is the girl with you?"

"No sir, I am alone."

"Do you know where she is?"

"No. I lost contact with her, but I have the flash drive."

"OK. Drive to the Intersection of Old Dominion Drive and Center Street. Look for the McLean Hair Center. Be there in one hour. There will be a black SUV parked at the rear of the building. Leave your keys in the car and enter the rear passenger door. Once inside, you will find written instructions. Follow them to the tee. We will speak later when this is all over. I admire your courage, Dr. Allen. Goodbye." Cam's hands are shaking as he places the phone in his pocket.

He waits until the appropriate time and makes the twenty-minute drive to the rendezvous location. His car pulls alongside the empty SUV. Leaving his keys behind, he enters the rear passenger door. As forewarned, there is a list of instructions. The first is to empty his pockets of all items, which he does. The second is to place the handcuffs on his wrists, and the third is to securely tie a blindfold around his head. He complies with all three. He sits in blackness for ten minutes and feels someone tug a hood over his head for added security. The car starts, and it begins to move. A tall man in a suit and close-cropped hair drives the vehicle aimlessly for forty-five minutes to disorient the passenger, leaving the Volvo for his nearly twin accomplice to dispose of.

Both parties meet at the driveway of a nondescript house on Scotts Lane once used by the CIA to shelter Soviet defectors. A musty smell, signifying years of limited usage, fills the air. The blindfolded passenger is led inside for debriefing. A needle is thrust into his neck before the hood and blindfold are removed, and he is carried into the back room. The handcuffs are opened, and he is shackled to a loose chain that is bound to the floor. When he awakens, he will have some freedom of movement.

The two agents guarding the man could be twins. Both maintain very short dark hair and wear black suits and white shirts under thin black ties. Each has the same reflective aviator sunglasses, appearing reminiscent of the lead characters in the movie Men in Black. One remains to guard the prisoner and keep him in isolation. The other is assigned to bring the recovered flash drive to the CEO of ParTek Industries.

They speak to each other.

"We have instructions to bring the flash drive immediately to Daniel Dryden and keep the prisoner here."

"I can't stand that pale geek. He is always so condescending. What the heck is he going to do with this? He can't even tie his own shoelaces. Why the hell are we dealing with that smug jerk, anyway?"

"The man says do it, and I do it. I'm not here to question. I follow orders and cash my paycheck. Anything else is a bonus. You're no rocket scientist yourself. You got any better ideas?"

"No, but if he gives me any lip, I'll be happy to put a bullet in his ear."

"Just do as you're told and keep your mouth shut."

Chapter 22

Thursday 3:00 PM, Penthouse ParTec Industries Old Dominion Drive & Lowell Ave, McLean, VA

Daniel is elated when he gets the knowledge the flash drive is back in the group's possession. His confidence and swagger returned. Holding it up to the light, he muses how something so small could be so valuable. The Chief IT Officer of ParTec has been brought in to examine it. He is instructed to check for any viruses that may have been secretly installed while it was outside of their control. He takes the valued object to his office to perform some tests. ParTec hired one of the best cybernetics experts in the country. A proud achievement Daniel never hesitates to boast. One hour later, he returns, declaring the data files to be safe.

They next contact Colonel Fielding at Fermi to advise him they may have the potential to once again proceed with the experimentation.

"That weasel Stanton secretly catalogued all fifteen grams of the stuff that was produced. We can't take any of it without sending off alarms from here to the White House," states the Colonel.

"We need to produce five more uncatalogued grams to meet our buyers' requirements. Do you think you can get that done, Colonel?" Dryden poses.

"Just start transferring the files here to me. I flew Dr. George Salazar in from Los Alamos on a military jet. He landed at Volk Field in Camp Douglas, WI, this morning. If anyone else can do this, he can. No one knows that he's here. He arrived at Fermi about an hour ago and is dealing with some jet lag, but I think we can get everything set to begin sometime tonight or tomorrow morning. The downside is that he is unfamiliar with our equipment and will need some time to get comfortable. It is also unfortunate that Dr. Millstead is no longer around to assist him. I have been told he's the brightest military scientist we have. Let's hope he meets the hype. It seems like there's a million of these geeky nerds walking the street with their microscopes, but the really good ones are rare and act like primadonnas."

Daniel scowls at the military man's ignorance. What the hell does that dinosaur know about science?

"Colonel, we are transmitting the files now. It may take some time. Please advise when the transfer is complete."

Daniel and Kristen prepare to exit for the dining room, but before they can leave, the screen illuminates, and the following words appear:

DO YOU HAVE THE FLASH DRIVE?

Daniel stops in his tracks and types quickly,

YES, WE JUST CHECKED IT FOR VIRUSES AND IT IS CLEAN. WE ARE TRANSMITTING THE FILES TO THE COLONEL NOW. HE HAS SOMEONE IN PLACE READY TO START THE PROCESS OVERNIGHT. WE MIGHT BE ABLE TO FINISH BEFORE DAYBREAK.

DON'T BE SO SURE, DANIEL DRYDEN. DR. ALLEN IS A VERY CLEVER MAN. I DON'T THINK THIS WILL BE SO EASY. WE MUST FIND THE GIRL. SHE IS THE LEVERAGE WE NEED TO FORCE HIS COMPLIANCE. FIND HER.

Daniel responds hesitantly:

YES, SIR, WE WILL GET RIGHT ON IT. SHE CAN'T HIDE FOREVER.

ENOUGH WTH THE PROMISES, DANIEL DRYDEN. I WANT RESULTS.

With that, the screen goes blank.

Kristen takes her brother's hand, and they walk across the hall to the dining room as he places a frantic call to his Asian mercenaries.

Chapter 23

Thursday 7:00 PM, The Canopy by Hilton, 975 7th Street, Washington, DC

The agents spent the remainder of the day obtaining a rental car and securing a place to spend the evening. They returned to both the Smithsonian and the Channel Apartments several times to see if anyone had heard from the missing Doctor. All the information accumulated on the Allen family was sent back to headquarters for the analysts to decipher.

Diane was a bit reclusive, seeming lost in thought. She knew they were being tracked, and it bothered her not to know who or how. It was now dinner time, and the three sat down to analyze the status of their investigation. They knew they were close but could not make that last leap. How come they weren't able to locate Cameron's brother's wife? Did she leave the area? A breakthrough was needed soon, or Dr. Allen would perish at the hands of the enemy.

They decide to walk down to Hanks Oyster Bar for alfresco dining with a view of the river. The hope was that scenery and a tasty meal would rejuvenate both their minds and their bodies. The banter lightened somewhat, and Diane kept staring at the obituary notice for Cameron's brother.

Roger's beverage ruled this roost, and the agents allowed him to select the opening round. They sipped frosty mugs of golden liquid as the plates of oysters and crabs continued to flow in.

The night was pleasant, and a plan was formulated in Diane's head. Roger knew that look, and he hoped he could get her drunk enough to abandon it. All she could dwell on was the missing final piece.

They took out the newspaper articles, sifting through them once again. This time, Diane noticed there was another fatality in the boating accident. A third unrelated article mentioned that a lawsuit was filed. Cam's brother was being sued for negligence. That is it. Run a check for properties in the name of Sandstrom. If they were being sued, chances are his widow either relocated or shifted the assets back into her name. If for no other reason than to avoid the publicity. They saunter back to the hotel lobby for a nightcap, and Brad's team comes back with:

Ursula Sandstrom

XXXX Hawkins Lane

Chevy Chase, MD.

"That's our next move, gentlemen. We go there first thing in the morning, got it?" Diane senses they are hot on the trail.

"And what time is that?" asks Brad.

"Let's all meet at her place at 10:00 AM. Give them time to wake up. I want two cars there in case we need to split up. Go home and get a good night's sleep, Brad. We will need you in the morning."

Brad makes his exit, and Roger stares at his partner. "What in the world are you cooking up? Why did you tell him 10 AM?

"We leave here at 7:30 AM. I want to find out who is following us and who is orchestrating it. We want him to arrive late. He will be the calvary."

"Isn't there a better way?"

"I'm all ears if you got one."

"I'll say this, Agent Vitullo, you got a pair."

They laugh and she goes a bit further into detail before they head back to their respective rooms.

"In field hockey we used to say, sometimes you got to take a hit to make a play."

"You're crazy, Vitullo," are the last words uttered as their doors slam shut."

Retiring inside her hotel room, Diane removes her shoes. She hated wearing heels, but a certain decorum was needed in her position. She rubbed her soles through their nylon encasement and sat on the sofa as her thoughts drifted back to that fateful night ten years ago. She remembers how happy her parents were when her uncle was promoted. They were working on a deep case involving millions of dollars in government theft. It had consumed them for the better part of eight months. The plan was sophisticated and elaborate. They suspected someone on the inside but could never muster any proof. It was similar in many respects to the case before her. Witnesses seemed to disappear, and evidence was hard to find. She mused at the commonalities she now faced.

She remembers waving to them as they left for dinner that night. She sat and watched with the headphones of her iPod in her ears. Diane never heard the last words her mother spoke.

"I owe you, Mom and Dad. My promise is to be the best. Tomorrow's plan is in your honor." With that, she kisses ever present wallet photo of the three of them hugging. A single tear escapes before she can close her eyes for the evening.

Chapter 24

Friday 2:00 AM, Fermi Lab., Batavia, IL

The download is complete, and in the current shift, all loyal appointees of the Colonel have control of the lab. Dr. Salazar has spent the last two hours becoming familiar with the delicate instruments and unique procedures. He keeps looking at the anomaly with awe, and the scientist in him would love to study it. He then looks down at the bars on his collar and remembers that he is a captain in the United States Army and must follow the orders of his superior officer.

The Colonel is tense, having given the powers to be his assurances that he could accomplish their goals and produce the necessary quantity of exotic material before the sun rises. A closed-circuit video feed of the experiment is being sent live to the offices of ParTec Industries in McLean, VA. He muses at the thought of Daniel and Kristen Dryden watching the video in bed. He snickers, maybe even the same bed. Something about those two was creepy.

In the decade they have been doing business, he has never seen either of them with a companion of the opposite sex. He longed for the day he was rid of their prying eyes. This payday would be their richest ever. His share comes to $15,000,000.00, dwarfing any previous haul of the past ten years. It was enough to spend the rest of his life on a beach in total luxury.

The machines are energized. Everything must occur in the proper sequence to achieve the frequencies and magnetic levels necessary to break down the strong nuclear force. Dr. Salazar begins the ten-step process by signaling the start of Phase I. Everything in the lab seems to buzz, and atoms are energized to the precise level. The magnetism needs to be raised. He calls out for Phase II and another level of activity takes place focused on the temperature.

The excitement and tension in the room rise to another level. Expectations heighten as the same process occurs for Phases III through V. They pause to allow everything to synchronize before going to the next step.

The Colonel closes his eyes, and his thoughts wander to Mai Tais on the shoreline in the company of scantily clad Asian teens. He looks down at the young Sergeant. She knew how to please him and never refused one of his unusual nighttime requests. Should he take her with him or play the youthful field? He is lost in thought, weighing the pluses and minuses of each option, when he hears Dr. Salazar call for Phase VI.

There is a sudden silence; everything pauses, and the unemotional voice of the computer fills the room.

"Please enter the password for Phase VI."

Dr. Salazar looks up, shrugging his shoulders, not knowing what to do next. His eyes beseeching the Colonel for the proper code. Thrown out of his erotic stupor, Fielding looks down at the physicist, unable to supply an answer.

"Colonel, what do you want us to do? We can't leave the system half charged very long."

"Shut it down," he replies.

They slowly back out of the process in the same systematic way it was begun. The Colonel, battling both rage and disappointment, feels his cell begin to buzz in his pocket. He reaches for it, knowing this is not going to be a pleasant call.

Chapter 25

Friday 4:00 AM, Penthouse ParTec Industries, Old Dominion Drive & Lowell Ave, McLean, VA

The sudden stoppage of activity at Fermi brings both executives up into the boardroom. Daniel's pajamas and robe droop loosely over his thin frame. In contrast, his sister sports a sexy nightgown, revealing an ample amount of her toned, tanned body. The taut lines are evidence of her dedication to the gym.

The mood is somber as Daniel attempts to telephone the Colonel, wanting an explanation. He needed answers before the big guy contacted him. Each knew there was hell to pay, and each wanted to ensure it was the other who paid it.

Not wanting his team to hear the conversation, Fielding returns to his office. Heated words are exchanged between the two men when Kristen interrupts.

"Cool it with the egos, men. That's not going to help us get to the bottom of this."

The Colonel takes the floor, explaining that Dr. Allen was somehow able to corrupt the flash disk to modify the program. It now requires at least one password to reach level VI. We are not certain if additional passwords are required for levels VII through X.

Daniel asks, "Why don't we just get Dr. Allen to the lab and threaten him until he gives up the codes?"

Kristen chimes in, "It seems that simple to me."

The Colonel responds, "We are dealing with a genius here. He knows we can't kill him because if he dies, the codes will be lost forever. Not cooperating is the only thing that ensures his survival."

Daniel is in a near panic. "Then what the hell do we do?"

Just as that question is posed, the screen begins to illuminate, and a collective shudder fills the room. The Colonel is ever so thankful not to be present.

CAN YOU TELL ME WHAT HAPPENED AT FERMI TONIGHT?

Daniel tries to grab the keyboard to respond but he is so nervous he nearly drops it on the floor. Kristen steps around him and, taking control, she enters the following:

DR. ALLEN SABOTAGED THE FLASH DRIVE. HE ALTERED THE PROGRAM BY INSERTING A PASSWORD. IT WAS ENCOUNTERED APPROACHING PHASE VI.

SMART MAN AND CRUEL LETTING YOU THINK IT WAS WORKING. I WARNED YOU NOT TO UNDERESTIMATE HIM.

Kristen keeps control and types:

WHY CAN'T WE SEND HIM TO FERMI AND FORCE HIM TO COOPERATE?

HE KNOWS THAT WE CAN'T KILL HIM. ONCE HE IS DEAD, WE LOSE THE CODES FOREVER. I ADMIRE HIS SAVVY. HE KNEW PROTECTING THE GIRL WAS KEY. SHE IS HIS ACHILLES HEEL. WE NEED TO APREHEND HER AS SOON AS POSSIBLE.

CAN'T WE DRUG HIM?

NO, THE DRUGS DON'T WORK LIKE THAT. WE NEED THE GIRL. DANIEL, ASSEMBLE YOUR MERCENARIES AND ADD THREE ADDITIONAL MEN TO THE TEAM. BE READY TO STRIKE ON A MOMENT'S NOTICE AT SUNRISE. YOU HAVE A TRACER ON THE AGENTS. THEY WILL LEAD YOU TO THE GIRL TOMORROW MORNING. REMEMBER, NO ONE GETS KILLED. THAT'S AN ORDER. WE CANNOT AFFORD ANY MORE HEAT ON THIS OPERATION. NEUTRALIZE THE ENEMY AND BRING HER TO THE SAFE HOUSE. HAVE YOUR PLANE READY FOR TAKE OFF ON MY SIGNAL. THE FIANCE IS HIS ONLY WEAK LINK. HE WILL COOPERATE TO PROTECT HER.

Kristen questions:

HOW CAN YOU BE SO SURE THE NSA AGENTS HAVE LOCATED HER?

I AM PRIVY TO WHAT THEIR ANALYSTS ARE SEEING. THEY HAVE DISCOVERED WHERE SHE IS HIDING. GET HER TO THE SAFE HOUSE AND BE READY TO MOVE THE PAIR QUICKLY.

The screen fades to black. With little chance of sleep, Daniel and Kristen stroll across the room to the bar and mix a pair of extraordinarily strong drinks.

Kristen looks at her brother with concern. A concern not for his wellbeing but rather one of his jeopardizing their operation. Her father was a cold, stern man but a good provider. They wanted for nothing as children. She does not know if the man sitting opposite her has the traits necessary to carry the enterprise into the next decade.

Chapter 26

Friday 8:00 AM, Hawkins Lane, Chevy Chase, MD

The rental car, having made the nearly eleven-mile trip north from the Canopy Hotel to Chevy Chase, pulls slowly into the long driveway of Hawkins Lane. It stops at the base near the roadway so as not to alarm those residing inside.

Diane grabs the door handle to exit, but before she can pull down on it, Roger's massive hand grips her other wrist.

"Are you absolutely certain you want to go through with this?"

"Roger, Dr. Millstead is dead because of me. I will not let another person perish. This is a matter of duty."

"That's crazy, Diane. You didn't force her to cooperate."

"No, but I got sloppy. I should have known we were being tracked. The signs were all there."

"Vitullo, I will march through hell with you, but you do not owe anyone anything. You are the best damn agent we got."

"Thank you, Roger, those are kind words, but I live by my own standards, and this will work. I am sure of it."

They exit the vehicle and walk to the entry, taking care not to startle those inside. They knock on the front door, holding their badges high. Ursula is already awake and hears the knock. She walks to the door to see who is there, and the agent's presence startles her. Diane sees her puzzled face through the glass and yells. "Ursula, please, we are here to help you. We know Pam is here. They are holding your brother-in-law captive. We need your help to save him."

Upon hearing this plea, she unlocks the door, opening it slightly to get a better look at the badges. Once her eyes confirm their validity, she allows the agents entry into the house. Standing down in the hall just inside a bedroom, a frightened Pamela peeks cautiously, trying to see who is speaking. Both women are already dressed in casual tops and jeans.

Diane sees her and turns, addressing the next words in her direction. "Ms. Ward, I am Agent Vitullo, and this is Agent Edwards. We need to speak with you. It is extremely important."

As Pamela leaves the bedroom and walks toward them, Diane notices that her hair has been cut short and dyed to a darker auburn hue, altering her image from the photo they were using.

Ursula invites all to sit down at the kitchen table. Diane knows that she should not rush into anything, but she is also aware her time is limited. She glances at her watch. Tea is offered and accepted by all. Ursula rises to prepare the kettle.

"Pamela, if I may," begins Diane, "we believe Cameron has been abducted by the same people Mark Stanton warned you about. I have a plan to rescue him and hopefully solve the problem at Fermi Lab, but we will need your help to accomplish that."

A cringing Pamela asks, "Is he okay?"

"We believe he is fine for now; they will not hurt him out of necessity. He is the only way to get their project back on track. However, we know they are looking for you, and we believe you can help us find Dr. Allen."

Both women train their eyes on the tall female detective, each asking themselves how.

"This is going to sound strange, but hear me out. First, I need Pam to swallow this pill. It is an untraceable and unremovable tracking beacon. We will be able to locate you for ninety-six hours until your digestive juices disintegrate the capsules." She hands one to the frozen woman opposite her. "This is a precaution in case you become separated from us. I know I do not have to elaborate on the ruthlessness of the people with whom we are dealing." Diane again peers at her watch, grateful that the pill has been ingested. She takes a sip of her tea and opens her mouth to continue.

Suddenly, both doors are kicked open, and five heavily armed assailants rush into the kitchen, holding the four at gunpoint. A remarkably familiar silhouette enters the room and shouts, "Hands up!" Diane stares straight into the face of a smirking Jun Li as she reaches in to remove the Glock from her holster. Their intense dislike for one another is apparent to all present.

"Hello, Detective American Bitch. So good to see you again."

"The feeling is mutual, Asian slut."

A quick thrust of Jun's right fist doubles Diane over. They relieve Roger of his weapon and tell the three to remain seated at the table. Instructions are given to zip-tie those seated to the chairs.

Diane, still standing, gathers her breath and asks, "Did it feel good to kill the doctor?"

"Killing always feels good, Detective American Bitch, and killing you will be the best feeling ever. I cannot wait for that moment."

Looking down at the shorter woman, Diane speaks again. "You little fiend, she was a frail, sickly scientist. Don't you feel tough?"

Jun Li responds nonverbally with another vicious blow into Diane's abdomen. The agent's shoulders lean forward, and she spits into the now irate face of the mercenary. The action is met with a throttling right fist to the jaw, snapping her head back with her dark hair flailing behind her as she stumbles back to the wall. It is quickly followed by an expertly thrown kick to the NSA agent's belly. She is now hunched over her buttocks, leaning against the wall, trying to inhale. Not content, Jun walks toward her and grabs the panting woman by her top, lifting and pressing her torso against the wall. Diane's legs dangle beneath her, and she clutches the back of her tormentor, hugging her for what seems like an extended moment. The action is broken when Li slams her groping adversary's head into the wall.

She releases her grip and allows the dazed body in front of her to slide down to the floor. She grabs her by the ankles and drags her to the center of the room. Zip ties are placed on her ankles and wrists, effectively immobilizing her. Wanting one final act of humiliation, she removes her shoe and presses her toes into the neck of her bound captive. Her dark nylons contrast with the agent's white skin. "Killing you will be ecstasy, American bitch. Until we meet again."

Using a knife, one of the other attackers frees one of the girls from her chair and drags her by the arms out of the house and into a running SUV. He hops into the passenger seat and awaits his partner's exit from the house. Chen Zhao waits for Jun Li in the other vehicle. On her way to meet him, she walks past the agent's rental car parked in the driveway and unholsters her gun to shoot holes in both front tires, thereby guaranteeing a smooth escape.

Back in the kitchen, Roger nervously yells over to Diane, "Are you okay?"

"It hurts like hell, but I'll live, I think."

"Did you do it?"

"Mission accomplished, Roger."

"I pity the asshole that puts a ring on that finger."

"Stop it, Edwards, it hurts when I laugh."

Approximately twenty minutes later, Detective Lieutenant Brad Jones's car speeds to a sudden stop in the driveway. With sidearm drawn, he rushes past the shattered entry and scampers into the house, where his eyes behold the alarming site. He sees Diane stretched out on the floor and a woman seated next to Roger in chairs, all zip-tied at the wrists and ankles.

"Don't just stand there, cupcake, cut us loose," barks an agitated agent Edwards.

Brad locates a pair of scissors and begins to free the seated captives first, saving Agent Vitullo for last. They all lean over her anxiously, looking to assess her injuries. Roger turns to ask Ursula for ice, and his jaw drops down to his chin.

"You're not going to believe this."

"What?" moans an aching Vitullo from a seated position on the floor.

"They took the wrong girl."

"What?"

He holds Diane up while a cold pack is applied to her jaw and another to her ribs and looks across the room to see an apoplectic Pam Ward sitting motionless at the table.

Trying to overcome the shock, Roger returns the focus to Diane's primary mission.

"Like I said, Vitullo, you have a pair. Where did you put it?"

"On her holster, the same place she put mine." They both laugh. "Stop it, Edwards, the American Bitch is hurting."

"Why the hell did you guys ice me? 10:00 AM seriously. You know, if I were here, I could have helped you."

"We didn't want you here. Then we needed you at 10:00 AM to free us, and we needed your car to leave."

"I don't understand this at all."

Diane reaches for his hand, "Do not worry, Brad, it will all become clear in the next few hours. One of you get my bag. Let's open my tablet and see if this was all worthwhile."

The screen lights up, and she sees a bright blue dot heading south across a map toward Virginia. A jubilant agent yells "Bingo" about as loud as her bruised ribs will allow.

They call the rental company to send out a tow truck for the damaged automobile and begin to leave. "Agents, why don't we all camp back at my townhouse? It has three bedrooms. We can operate from there as a base until we know what we got."

Diane says, "Good idea. Pam, you will need to come with us. We will protect you."

They pile into Brad's car, and Roger instructs him to drive to the nearest hospital. "She is hurting more than she is letting on."

The group makes a slight detour, dropping a protesting Agent Vitullo off one hour later at AmeriHealth Caritas Medical Center on Maryland Ave. Roger, Brad, and Pam go to the Canopy by Hilton to check out of their rooms and bring their belongings to Detective Jone's abode. They promised Diane they would return to pick her up when finished.

Chapter 27

Friday 11:00 AM, Safe House Scotts Run, McLean, VA

Dr. Cameron Allen finds himself alone in a windowless room. There are two chairs. He is shackled to one with a long chain. He has enough slack to stand up and wall around the table but not enough to touch any of the walls. There is a small refrigerator, just barely within reach. It is filled with icy water. The room is not dark but could use a little brightening.

He rubs his eyes, trying to wipe out the sleepy malaise that engulfs him. "They must have drugged me on arrival." He shuffles to the refrigerator, accompanied by the clanging noise of a dragging chain. His lips are parched, and his throat is dry. He needs the water to soothe both. His watch is gone, and he has no clue of the time or how long he has been out. He swallows the chilly tonic, thankful that the hood and blindfold are gone.

As soon as the cool refreshment hits his tongue, he hears the only door to the room open. In walks a tall, fit man, a mirror image of his accomplice wearing the same black suit. The white shirt and thin black-tie date him to the 1960s. He removes his sunglasses and sits at one end of the table. He motions for the Doctor to sit opposite him, and Cam complies.

"Time for a little chat, Dr. Allen, is it?"

Still disoriented, the fog in his head begins to dissipate. He recalls the ritualistic rendezvous and the strict rules he was given.

"Did you not realize that we would learn the flash drive was altered?

"On the contrary, I was counting on it."

"Is that some kind of joke?"

"No, sir, this is a very serious matter. More serious than you people realize. The potential danger you are risking is epic."

"We need the original flash drive. Just tell us where it is, and we will let you go."

"You'll never get the drive from me, and without me, your goose is cooked."

"Doctor, don't you understand we will stop at nothing to finish this mission? Your life is inconsequential to us. We have no problem ending it if you do not help us."

"All I know is that you cannot succeed without me, and killing me only ensures your failure. My terms are that I deal with the anomaly first and help you finish your mission afterward. When I am convinced the world is safe, I'll do everything in my power to help you."

"Doctor, I am trying to reason with you. This is not a negotiation. Give us what is ours, and you can go back to your beloved Institute."

"Do I look naïve, sir? The minute you get what you want, I am history. You know that as well as I do. He cannot let me live now that I know he is involved."

The interrogator's next line is interrupted by the buzzing of his phone.

"I'll be right back."

Cameron Allen is left alone to think about his circumstances, figuring he can at least fashion a stalemate. His mind wanders to the lovely blonde with big blue eyes that stole his heart. Gosh, his timing sucked. He broods that he has no access to her. The track phone he had taped to his ankle must have been found during their search. The only remains of its existence are small pieces of duct tape dangling from his pant leg. Cam struggles to hear the conversation in the next room, stretching the chain to its maximum and leaning forward to get as close as possible. The conversation ends, and he rushes back to his seat.

"Well, Dr. Allen, the deck has been reshuffled. The girl has been located, and she is in our custody. We expect her to arrive in an hour or two. I just love reunions, don't you? Why don't we break now and resume when she arrives?

After a long pause, "Life's a bitch isn't it, Doc?"

It is all Cameron can do to hide the reaction percolating within him. *"Be strong, Cam, be strong. You can't let them see she gets to you. Your weakness will doom us both."*

Chapter 28

Friday 1:00 PM, AmeriHealth Caritas Medical Center, 1250 Maryland Av SW, Washington, DC

They watch the mercenaries' icon head back across the state line and into northern Virginia. The car appears to stop at a building on Old Dominion Drive located somewhere between the restaurant she dined at with her 'Uncle' and the hotel where she spent the evening. Diane is amused at the coincidence. She gives Roger and Brad the address and requests they research the building owners and tenants to see if anything warrants a closer look.

"We got a ton of work to do tonight. Pick up a handful of pads and pens along with a whiteboard. I know we are close, and I suspect this is big."

Diane has made a conscious decision not to get the DC office involved. This will ensure confidentiality but will deprive them of valuable resources. Painfully, the agent exits the car and walks gingerly into the emergency room. She will not give her employment status to the staff, preferring to avoid hours of red tape and piles of reports. An ER nurse meets her in the lobby just as Roger turns to leave. He promises a hasty return. Her partner is very disturbed by the strategy she selected, but deep down inside, they both know she did the right thing even though the pain she is experiencing argues to the contrary.

She is asked the usual questions and given a form to fill out. Providence is on her side as the emergency room is empty, and there is no one else in the waiting area. Once the form is completed and returned to the nurse, she is ushered into a small stall, and the curtain is drawn. She is handed the standard hospital gown and asked to remove her jacket and blouse. Her gun and holster are hidden inside her suit coat, and the gown is tied around her body.

A young black nurse reads her chart and administers it to her by checking her vitals. She cringes when she sees the bruising on Diane's ribs.

"Did you get hit by a truck or fight Mike Tyson," she jokes.

"Feels like I did both," whimpers Diane, forcing a smile.

Just then, the doctor walks in, tall and handsome. His eyes lock with Diane's, and the two engage in a lengthy stare. He appears to be in his early to mid-thirties with dark hair and magnificent eyes. His warm smile melts the hardened detective as she feels her toes curl. The connection between the two is both instant and intense. She thinks he is blushing and wonders if she is doing the same.

He opens by saying, "Let's take a look at those." Realizing his error as soon as it exits his mouth, he tries to recover, stuttering quickly to remedy his faux pas, "Ribs, I mean."

To ease the tension, Diane counters with, "Only if your hands aren't cold, Doctor."

"Call me Dr. Parisi, and after the last comment, you should understand that I am not very cool."

There's laughter in the small examination area, and both parties are impressed by the others' wit. He performs the standard examination and orders a set of X-rays.

"I want to take a closer look at those ribs, but my preliminary diagnosis is that one or two are cracked. The only medication I can prescribe are pain pills. The ribs should heal naturally but you will be experiencing close to this level of pain for several more days."

The patient is led to radiology, and while she is away, Roger returns to the hospital and searches for Diane. The ER nurse asks if he is her husband. Roger responds in the negative.

"No, we are business partners and good friends."

The doctor seems pleased to hear this, holding back a grin.

The X-rays are taken and read quickly, and the original diagnosis is confirmed. He hands her an envelope containing two Percocets and a script for more.

"We could tape the ribs, but it really does not help much. The tape can also be painful to remove."

Agent Vitullo graciously thanks the fine-looking male specimen, getting lost in his eyes once more.

"Here's my card. Call me anytime, day or night, if the pain increases."

She accepts the card, gazing at his hands to see if there is a ring on his third finger. The moment lingers until Roger coughs, breaking the silence.

A flurry of activity at the entrance has the medical professionals rushing off to tend to the next emergency. That leaves Roger alone to assist Diane back to Detective Jones's car.

During the short ride back, she senses Roger's uneasiness. Trying to console him, she says, "Roger, aside from the pain, I'm fine."

"I should not have let you do this, Diane. I felt so helpless while you were being worked over."

"The stakes are high, partner. Let's make sure it wasn't done in vain."

Chapter 29

Friday 4:00 PM, Jones Residence 4th Place. SW, Washington, DC

Brad and Pam stroll to the Safeway Supermarket on Fourth Street to stock up with supplies. He anticipates a long night. They return to the house and are in the process of unpacking when Roger pulls the car into the garage below them. The powerful man gently assists his partner up the narrow staircase and into the living room. They carefully remove her jacket and her shoulder holster making sure to minimize her motion. She is eased into the recliner, and her legs are elevated. Diane, ever eager to kick off her heels, sheds them on the carpeted floor. Roger places a blanket over her torso and thighs.

"Nice place here, Brad. How long have you been living here?"

"I have owned it for a year but have been living here about six months. It needed a fair amount of renovations."

Brad heads to the kitchen with Pam to begin preparing dinner. To appease the lunch-deprived crew, they offer a charcuterie board and an assortment of beverages. Roger consumes a large cold beer while Diane and Brad sip red wine. Pam sticks with her favorite Pinot Grigio. The other three look to Diane to set the evening's agenda.

"This is going to be a long night, so I think we all should enjoy a nice dinner and then get to work. Brad, is there any feedback on the building owner?"

"The building is owned by ParTec Industries, and they are the sole occupant."

"That is good. It saves us a lot of hunting. Who owns ParTec Industries?"

"That would be one Daniel Dryden, age 34, and his sister Kristen, age 32. They are the sole owners, but I am not certain of the split. Both are single and never married. The company was founded by their father, Gunther Dryden, in early 2008."

Diane feels as though that name is familiar, but she cannot be certain, so she keeps her reaction hidden.

"Seems like it floundered for the first few years, but in 2014, the profits soared through the roof. Most, if not all, of their business is government-related, either to the US or foreign entities. It is privately held, so there are not a whole lot of public financials."

Roger interjects, "If they were doing government work, we should be able to track the business with other filings. I can make a couple of calls and see what shakes out. If we find something that gives us probable cause we can subpoena their tax returns."

"Great start, guys now please tell us what is cooking for dinner. Nothing builds an appetite like getting your ass kicked."

Roger smiled; he so admired his partner's intellect but her ability to laugh at herself was her real charm.

"It's a surprise. Eat your charcuterie and let the chef continue with his masterpiece."

The spread of meat, cheeses and assorted vegetables is devoured in minutes and a second round of drinks is poured.

Sipping her second glass of wine, Diane asks, "Brad, how many computers do you have?"

"I have a PC and a laptop."

Pam interjects, "I took my laptop as well."

"Good, that makes four counting my own."

"After dinner I will ask Pam if she would be agreeable to research anything she can about Mr. Gunther Dryden. I want info from the time his ass was spanked until they shoveled his grave. Will you do that, Pam?" Diane senses that Gunther may be a key piece to this puzzle.

"Happily," is the reply. "Anything I can do to help. They used to call me the 'terminal-ator' in med school. I was a legend for my research prowess."

"Good, Roger, you work your magic with your contacts as you always do. Get me a picture of what went on. Anything we could take to a judge."

"On it, partner."

"Oh, and I hate to give you double duty, but we need to get everything we can on Colonel pompous ass at Fermi. He is there for a reason, and we need to know why. I figure you are the best source for this info."

"That would be my pleasure. I despise that blowhard. Anything I can do to take that asshole down would be free of charge, even if I could charge you."

"Good. Brad, it would be most helpful if you could reach out to your local contacts to get info on the property. Any violations, inspections, alterations, or permits. Find us something that could get us inside without raising any suspicions."

"I'll get right on it when I take off my chef's hat."

"Okay. One more item of importance before we dine. Yummm, that aroma is intoxicating. We are all aware they have snatched the wrong hostage. Soon, they will realize that as well. Once they do, they will resume their efforts to find the real Pamela Ward. Remember, they still have a tracer on me. What they do not know is we are also tracing them. If they move toward us before we are ready, we must be prepared to evacuate at a moment's notice. It is important everyone gets that. I am hoping to avoid a hasty retreat, but any plan we formulate will need a bit of time to execute."

At that moment, Chef Brad announces that dinner is ready. Diane was assisted to her feet by Pam and Roger, and she was brought to a chair in the kitchen. A roast pork loin is placed at the center of the table, smothered in onions and peppers. It is served along with mashed potatoes, gravy, and black-eyed peas.

For the next thirty minutes, silence rules. The famished team gnaws its way to satisfaction, eating about everything in sight. The dessert is a pan of apple pie served with vanilla ice cream. Detective Jones has indeed outdone himself.

Trying to ingratiate himself with Roger, Brad offers to pour him an eighteen-year-old Macallan.

"Neat or rocks," he asks.

Roger responds with, "One cube." Brad pours two and walks over to hand the glass to him.

He begins to sit down when Agent Edwards quips, "Cupcake, you're going to make some lucky guy a great wife one day."

That comment raises a roar in the room as all those present, including Brad, double over with laughter. Anyone who underestimates Roger's sense of humor does so at their own peril.

After a brief digestive period, each set about the task at hand.

"Let's break at eleven and compare notes."

In addition to her focus on the investigation, Diane realizes she needs to report to her supervisor tomorrow morning so that she can extend their stay and continue the investigation. That conversation will be critical. She has known Myles now for several years, and he has always been fair, introspective, and deliberate. He also offered sound advice. Myles, however, was a rule follower, something Diane found tedious at best. Her decision not to inform the DC office of their operation will be a tough one to sell. She hopes she is up for the task.

Chapter 30

Friday 7:00 PM, Safe House, Scotts Run Rd., McLean, VA

Cameron has been dealing with a heavy heart since he learned Pam was located and abducted. He hears the front door open and footsteps leading to an adjoining room. A sense of self-loathing fills his soul. Pam has been betrayed. Done in by the inflated ego of two men, each thinking they were much smarter than they were. How bold of him to think he could survive in this shadowy world, having never been exposed to it before. His only goal now was to spare her life. Nothing else mattered, not even his own.

An hour or two passes while he basks in his own misery. Finally, there is activity and movement in the adjacent room. The door to his chamber opens and a hooded figure is led inside to the table where he is seated. The figure is obviously female. She is shackled in the same manner as him. He realizes that he will soon be able to hug her and hold her while he apologizes profusely for his arrogance.

The man who interrogated him walks in behind her.

"We know how important she is to you, Dr. Allen. No need to try and hide it. We have taken an extra precaution to ensure that she has not seen any of us. This will hopefully convince you of our willingness to free her after you assist us. We will not harm her."

Cam's brain tries to digest all of this while trying to manage his raging heart. The woman he now knows he loves is sitting right across from him. Her potential fate was squarely in his hands.

"So, what do you say, Doctor?"

"Can you give us some time together to speak before I answer you?"

"Why, certainly, we are not savages. When I leave, feel free to remove her hood. When I do return, I will hide my identity. We want you to believe us. Our proposition is a fair one, Dr. Allen. You will not find a better option."

His captor leaves, and the viability of their offer begins to warm. Anything that saves Pam's life is fine with him. Damn Stanton's experiment, all he cares about is the blue-eyed angel that stole his heart. He shuffles to the other side of the table and begins to remove the dark hood concealing the head of his co-captive. He tugs it off, and his heart stops. Cam stares down into the wide-eyed face of his sister-in-law. She is the only person more perplexed than he is right now. Cam knows their captors are monitoring them and begins a command performance worthy of an Oscar.

He shouts, "Who are you? Where's Pamela? What kind of sick joke is this.?"

He is overly loud and overly animated, hoping Ursula gets the message. They have only one chance to make this work. They must convince the jailers they are strangers.

The door opens with a startled guard rushing inside wearing a ski mask covering his face.

"What are you trying to do here, you bastard? Didn't you think I would know?" He magnifies his outrage, trying to sell the ploy.

"What do you mean, Dr. Allen?"

"Look at her that's not Pamela Ward. You buffoon, do you not have her picture? What kind of game are you running here?"

He makes every move now with the intent of keeping his captors on the defensive.

The masked man looks at Ursula and asks, "Who are you?"

She responds by giving him her birth name, which is indeed on her driver's license. A quick call is made, and Pam's photo is emailed. He looks down at it and up at Ursula, holding the photo as close to her as possible. Similarities aside it is quite clear they do not have the right woman in custody. The ever-calm inquisitor now makes a panicked rush to the phone to spread the word. He is certain heads will roll when the higher-ups learn what happened.

When everyone leaves the room and they are both alone, Cam gives his sister-in-law a wink coupled with a thumbs up. Her brief but compelling performance may have just saved both of their lives.

Chapter 31

Saturday 9:00 AM, Penthouse ParTec Industries, Old Dominion Drive & Lowell Ave, McLean, VA

The top floor of the Dominion Drive building is split between the residence of the two principals and the corporate boardroom. This sunny Saturday morning finds the two in the common dining area of the residential portion. A morning breakfast prepared by their personal chef is brought to the table on domed plates. The lids are removed to reveal a piping hot plate of eggs benedict with hashed brown potatoes. Both siblings smile as the scent of their gourmet breakfast fills their nostrils. Daniel's day is scheduled for a chess match with his computer, while Kristen looks forward to a lengthy gym session. Today is a weight day. She loves pushing her body to the limit. It will be followed by a sparring session kickboxing with her trainer.

They have been given word that the scientist's fiancé was located and is now in custody inside a safe house. The Asian mercenaries in their employ located and apprehended the woman yesterday. She was handed to her partner's operatives for processing. This will be a feather in their cap. The two killers seem to be earning their pay in spades.

Kristen is just a bit jealous. She regrets having to hand off what she perceives as fun duties to a third party. Forced by her brother to play the executive role, she does her best to adapt. She readily admits that it is very boring. The younger Dryden had a lust for violence, but she was now forced to get her kicks in the gym. A smile washes over her face, remembering the thrill of her first kill over a decade ago. Face painted black and disguised in ragged clothes, and they decimated their targets in a most violent way. She loved handling this important job for their father and his partner. It was their initiation into the fold. And they passed with flying colors. Truth be told, Kristen did the bulk of the work while her brother turned pale and nearly vomited. The exhilaration was unequaled. Pure violence excited her so. Daniel, on the other hand, was weak and found it utterly distasteful. She thought he was going to be sick. Father always knew this, and subsequent actions were given to her to handle alone. She was damn good at it. The joy of the kill excited her so. The sensation was way more pleasurable than any elation she had ever received from a man in her bed.

Breakfast was halfway completed when the unnatural buzzing of their boardroom screen filled the room. This noise was the signal of only one caller. The mysterious partner they know only as "Ice." The servants understood what was happening, and they replaced the stainless-steel domes with the half-eaten breakfast plates. There would be a temporary pause in the meal.

Daniel and Kristen rose, walked across to the boardroom, and closed the door. They sat and looked up at the screen, anxiously awaiting the purpose of this unexpected call.

DANIEL DRYDEN, DO YOU TAKE ME FOR A FOOL?

Stunned, the CEO responds,

NO, SIR, I DON'T UNDERSTAND. WHY ARE YOU ASKING THIS?

WE REQUESTED YOU TAKE THE LEAD TO LOCATE PAMELA WARD AND DELIVER HER TO MY AGENTS.

YES, SIR, OUR MERCENARIES LOCATED HER BY TRACKING THE NSA AGENTS TO THE TARGET. SHE WAS TAKEN FROM THE SITE AND DELIVERED TO YOUR EMISSARIES.

ARE YOU AWARE, DANIEL DRYDEN, THAT THE WOMAN YOU DELIVERED IS NOT THE ONE WE SEEK? HOW COULD YOU BE SO INEPT?

WHAT ARE YOU SAYING? IT CAN'T BE.

THE QUESTION IS NOT WHO SHE IS BUT WHO SHE IS NOT.

WE DO NOT KNOW HOW THIS COULD HAPPEN. WE PROMISE TO GET TO THE BOTTOM OF IT.

THE WOMAN WE HAVE IN CUSTODY PROVIDES NO INCENTIVE FOR THE DOCTOR TO COOPERATE. WE NEED PAMELA WARD AND WE ARE GIVING YOU FORTY-EIGHT HOURS TO PRODUCE HER. DO YOU UNDERSTAND? OUR BUYERS ARE BECOMING IMPATIENT. NO MORE EXCUSES.

DON'T WORRY, SIR. WE ARE STILL TRACKING THE AGENTS, AND MOST LIKELY, THE WOMAN IS STILL WITH THEM. WE WILL FIX THIS.

YOU HAVE FORTY-EIGHT HOURS TO DO SO. A SECOND FAILURE WILL NOT BE TOLERATED.

With that, the screen fades to black.

Daniel is trembling so much that he can hardly open his desk drawer to fetch the vial of pills he so desperately needs. Kristen hands him a water bottle. "We need to have a chat with Ms. LI as soon as possible."

A call to the mercenaries is initiated and the two await a response.

Shortly after noon, the call was returned. Jun Li's lone face appears on the screen, and she asks the purpose of the call. Daniel is beside himself.

"You are blithering idiots. Do you know you captured the wrong girl? How can you be so stupid?"

"Mr. Dryden, sir, we captured the blonde as per our instructions. It is not our fault that all white people look alike."

"Well, I am ordering you to fix this now. You have forty-eight hours to bring me the girl. Do you understand that?"

"That should not be a problem, Daniel. The agent's whereabouts are still known. However, it will cost you, Daniel Dryden. If you agree to pay, we will strike today and bring you the girl in the time allotted."

A desperate CEO agrees to the new terms.

The screen goes black once again, and Kristen turns to her brother. "You should have let me oversee that, brother. I so hate sitting on the sidelines getting bullied by these Asians when they get to have all the fun."

"We are executives now, Kristen. We no longer get our hands dirty. We hire people to perform those tasks. They take all the risk."

Daniel looked at his sister, whom he loved dearly, but that love had always been tempered by fear. Her eyes were cold, like that of a shark, and she lacked emotion. Deep down inside, he wondered if she really enjoyed killing.

Chapter 32

Saturday 10:00 AM, NSA Headquarters, Undisclosed location, Chicago, IL

Myles Warner is not much of a detective. He achieved his rank and position because of his managerial skills. He was an organizer, a man of details, and a motivator. But even though he possessed none of the skills inherent in a great detective, he knew one when he saw one. His ability to recognize this talent was his finest trait. During his forty years of service, he saw a ton of agents come and go. He started and moved to Treasury and ended up here with the NSA. He knew Dianes' parents from his early days at the FBI as a profiler. Even though both were excellent agents, Diane Vitullo was the best natural detective he had ever encountered. She possessed the right combination of wits, guts, and intuition, all wrapped up in an attractive package. She never failed to impress him.

Even so, she had a whole lot of explaining to do to make sense of the last few days. He always gave his good agents the benefit of the doubt. There would be no exception in this case. However, the extreme nature of her latest moves caused him to wonder a bit more than usual. He needed to hear the rationale behind some of these radical decisions. Why was normal protocol avoided? The sting of the DC office calling to chew him out was still burning inside him. Why were they running an operation in their territory without prior notification? His ass was so sore he now needed a cushion to sit in his office chair.

Myles did his best to fend it off but even he was not sure why it happened. He was getting too old for this. At last, the phone rings and the speaker button is activated. Agent Vitullo is on the line. His questions would be answered.

"Sir, good morning. I hope everything is well with your health."

"Well, I am fine except for my raging ulcer. The one that you are doing your best to inflame. Thanks to you, I am sitting in a dark room on burning hot coals, forced to drink from a carton of milk."

"I am so sorry, sir, but events have unfurled quickly, and we have been trying to stay current and meet the challenges. It has been a whirlwind."

"Enlighten me, detective."

"Okay, sir. Let me begin by stating my reason for not contacting the local office. We have circumstantial evidence that they were compromised. It may not be an agent, more likely an analyst, but information was leaked.

Our status is that we have located the fiancé, and she is in our custody. We believe Dr. Allen is being held by them but do not feel he will cooperate unless they can use the girl. Our number one suspect is ParTec Industries out of McLean, Virginia. They are involved with a crooked Colonel now running the lab at Fermi. We know they have someone up high guiding them, but we have no clue as to who it may be at this point.

"So, what is your plan, and how quickly can you act?"

Our plan is to neutralize the two Asian mercenaries working for ParTec. We believe they murdered Dr. Millstead. Once we neuter them, we can go inside and apply just the right amount of pressure to force a mistake. They have profited dramatically through government contracts, so we are also trying to track the money. We hope to have all the info we need by tomorrow and approach them on Monday morning. Roger is using his plethora of military contacts to get us additional info. With any luck, the DC operation will be shuttered by week's end. We can get a brief completed by Tuesday with a warrant to follow. We can then head back to Chicago to take care of the Colonel and the anomaly."

"Given the current state of the operation, I will let you proceed, Vitullo. But listen to me, and listen to me good. Under NO circumstances are you to go to a District Judge to get a warrant without letting the local office know beforehand. Do you understand me, agent?"

"Yes sir, I will follow your order to a "t" sir."

"Thank you, agent. My ulcer is most happy to hear those words. Now tell me the details of the neutering operation."

Diane goes into the details of her plan, discussing the personnel involved and the timing. She explains why it must be managed in the manner stated.

"Clever move, agent, but be careful. You have civilians at risk."

"That is understood, sir. We think we have planned for every contingency. They are not aware that we have a tracer on them. They are also unaware we found the tracer they placed on me. That tracer led them to Dr. Millstead. It is something I will never forget."

"What do you know about the owners of ParTec Industries?"

"They are both heirs. Siblings in their early thirties. The were handed the business from their wealthy father. We think they are soft white-collar criminals, which is why they hired the mercenaries. Once we get them face to face, we can apply some pressure and hopefully get them to make a mistake. The possibility exists that they may lead us up the chain as well. We are this close, sir; I can feel it, and Roger agrees."

"You missed your calling, agent. You should have been a lawyer or a politician. You may proceed under the caveat I laid out. Do not let me down."

"I never have, sir, and I don't intend to start now. Agent Vitullo out."

"I am happy to hear that, agent. Goodbye for now."

Diane and Roger share a glance, "A hospital? Really? Are you out of your mind?"

"No. Roger, I spoke to Doctor Will this morning. I came clean as to who we are. As luck would have it, he is a hospital trustee, and the fourth floor is vacant due to some pending renovations. I told him how valuable it would be to his country and then promised I would owe him immensely."

"Yeah, he's doing it for the red, white and blue."

"We need to get busy. They will be making hay to find the girl soon, and I do not want them to come here. I need to get to the hospital as soon as possible so they think I am hurting."

"And you're not?"

"No comment, Edwards, but I will say this, taking that bitch down will greatly speed up the healing."

Chapter 33

Saturday 1:00 PM, AmeriHealth Caritas Medical Center, 1250 Maryland Av. SW, Washington, DC

Diane awakens from a restless night. Sleep was fleeting. She kept thinking about today's operation and all the things that could go wrong. She also second guessed herself on getting Doctor Dreamy involved. Was it the right thing to do?

On the right side of her ledger was the necessity to take out these two ruthless mercenaries. It was the mandatory first move in going after ParTec, Industries. She also had the murder of Dr. Millstead weighing heavily on her mind. It was a rare occurrence when strategy and vengeance aligned.

She rises from the recliner that is her makeshift bed and heads to the bathroom to shower and dress.

Detective Jones is already awake and is pacing in the kitchen. This would be his first taste of real action. She hoped he was up to the task. He hands her a cup of coffee, and without uttering a word, he tries to give her some additional assurance.

Dressed and caffeinated, she gingerly walks down the steps and into the garage. Brad holds the passenger door open as she slowly bends into the seat. He walks around to the driver's side and gets in. The car pulls out and heads to the hospital, just a short drive away. On the ride over to their destination, the agent once again mulls over the endless details of her plan, searching feverishly for a flaw. She is convinced that they are on the right path. Outside, Diane and Brad are met by the female plainclothes officer he assigned to the job. Her role was to be Diane's roommate. A fellow patient. Brad makes the introductions, and they walk inside to meet Dr. Parisi. Agent Vitullo gasps. She could not believe her eyes. Is it possible that he can look even better today than on the day of their first meeting? She tries to compose herself, feeling a bit weak in the knees.

"Doctor, thank you so much for assisting us. You are doing a favor for me and a great service to your country."

"Diane, you can call me Will or Bill, okay? And I am happy to help but if I thought this would put any patients in danger, I would not have approved."

"I understand your position and admire it, Will. We are fortunate that the renovation you have scheduled does not begin until next week. Believe me, it is not our intention to put any more people in jeopardy."

"Great, then we are all on the same page. Follow me." He walks them to the elevator and takes them up to the fourth floor. She internally battles the sudden flush feeling of being in his presence. It is as if she has reverted to an awkward teenager.

"Feel free to select any of the rooms on this floor."

Diane looks around carefully and chooses one in the center of the hallway. It would provide ample notice of an attack from either direction.

"Can we relocate these two beds to that room?"

"Of course, let me help you."

The four wheel the beds inside the room and arrange them as they would in a functioning hospital room. Miscellaneous equipment is added to enhance the room's appearance. The setting is an important part of the plan.

"This will be your bed, officer, Candace, is it?"

"Yes, but please call me Candy."

"Okay, Candy, the plan is for you to put on the gown and have your pistol drawn under the blanket; I will do the same. Pamela will sit there. They are coming for her. Roger will be hiding in the bathroom. Brad will rush the door on our signal."

Diane had wanted Roger to stay back and guard Pam just in case the Asians made a move before they were ready. She missed his presence and had to continue without it. She trusted his input like no other, but there was also no one better qualified to keep Pam safe until everything was set in motion.

"Detective Jones, you need to get back and be ready to bring Ward and Agent Edwards here on command. We should also do a sound check before you leave."

Dr. Parisi marvels at the statuesque beauty's ability to take charge and consider multiple contingencies. She appears sexier to him by the minute. Who is this whirlwind that came limping into my life?

"Will, you better scoot. I will contact you when this is all over. Go somewhere safe. I do not want you anywhere near harm's way. But before you go, I want to tell you again how much I appreciate what you are risking here."

"I am a decent judge of people; the risk is manageable. But you better not leave here without saying goodbye." He puts his hand on her shoulder, and she nearly melts. "Diane, please be careful."

"I'll do my best."

At that very moment, a black SUV rolls into the parking lot and pulls into a spot with a clear visual line to the entrance.

Jun Li speaks, "The American agent has returned to the hospital. Seems my little greeting was a bit too aggressive." Laughter follows. "We wait for the girl to enter. They will bring her here. It is the right tactical move for them. They are unaware of my tracking device. This will be an easy snatch."

"How do you know she will come?" questions Chen.

"The safest strategy for them is to group together. They will bring her. You wait and see."

"We only have forty-eight hours. Don't you think we are wasting time here?" protests Chen.

"Do not question me, Zhao. I understand their mindset. She will be here, I guarantee it."

When Diane's tracker shows the mercenaries to be stationary in the parking lot, she calls Roger and gives him the signal to head on over. "They are in the lot, staking us out. Once they are certain Pam is here, they will make their move."

Brad drives the two from his house back to the hospital, pulling in tight to the entrance opening to lessen the risk of an exterior ambush. The two exit the vehicle quickly and stride furtively to the elevators. When the doors close, Brad pulls away to meet up with his uniformed officers. They watch the parking lot, huddled in a van across the street.

Upstairs on the fourth floor, Roger and Pam enter the room. Diane is relieved when her partner arrives on time.

He greets Diane, "So you want me in the bathroom?

"But you can leave your pants on."

"I will get you for this."

"Find the best spot in there where you can spring into action. For anyone to leave, they must get by you."

"Diane, I do not need another reason to put a bullet in the little bitch's forehead. Jail is too good for her."

"Understood, Roger, understood."

"Pam, please go to the window and sit in that chair on the opposite side of the room near my bed. I need you to stay calm. We have every exit covered. Trust me. Everything is going to be all right. Can you do that for me?"

Pamela Ward nods and does what she is told, her palms sweating.

Diane calls Brad, "Are you getting the sound feed?"

"Loud and clear, agent."

"Good. Once we get what we need, you can rush to the door. Roger will spring from the bathroom, and we will pull out our weapons from the bed. We will have them in a crossfire."

"Looks like we are all set, Agent. Please be careful."

Diane and Candace quickly strip off their top clothing and put on the hospital gowns. Then, the two hastily climb into their respective beds with their firearms in place under the blankets. Diane makes one final check on the recorder, and the last piece is in place. All that remains is the wait. They lie patiently, trying to look calm as butterflies flutter inside their chests.

"Now we wait."

The thought of Dr. Millstead's death is prominent in her head. Diane feels responsible, and it gives her all the incentive she needs to punish these fiends. If needed, the pain in her ribs adds extra motivation. She listens over the pounding of her heart.

The wait was not a long one as the two assassins pressured for a quick result exit from the SUV. Chen Zhao possesses a syringe filled with enough drugs to put the pert blonde out for twenty-four hours. Their plan is to wheel her out on a gurney.

They enter the hospital lobby and look around for a storeroom where they can change. Minutes later, they emerged clad in hospital scrubs.

Once Brad sees the doors to the SUV open, their targets walk to the entrance. He pulls around into the lot, making sure to keep a safe distance behind.

"Diane, they are on their way."

"Understood." Diane relays this information to all in the room.

Roger leans against the bathroom wall, gun in hand, poised to strike, while Pam fidgets nervously in her chair.

The scrub-clad Asians confiscate a gurney in the lobby and wheel it into the elevator. Jun Li looks at her phone to make sure they know where their target sits. They go up slowly, one floor at a time, until they reach level four. This signal is clear. She is on this floor. They push off the elevator, following the pulse of her phone until they identify the correct room.

When enough time elapses for the assassins to reach the fourth floor, Brad enters the building and orders two of the uniformed police officers to remain in the lobby. No one is permitted to exit until the operation is finished.

He motions to the other two to follow him up the stairs to the fourth floor. They wait in the stairwell, listening attentively.

Diane lies under the blanket, trying to calm herself. She cannot wait for another encounter with her nemesis.

The tension is thick.

Chen Zhao stands at the entrance. "Let's move."

The door is already half open when they rush through, weapons bared. They see the two patients lying quietly in bed and their target on the far side of the room.

Chen shouts, "Nobody moves." He inches to the center of the room, a pistol drawn, keeping eyes on both beds. Jun walks further in and directly to Diane.

"Hello, Agent Bitch, glad to see you again." Her smirking air of superiority is evident.

Diane looks up into the muzzle of her weapon, "I wish I could say the same, but I have had my fill of you. Asian slut."

"Very funny, Agent Bitch. But not nice. I even came here to visit you in the hospital, and you treat me like this. I thought we were friends. But to be honest, I am not here for you; I have come for the girl. I'm going to take her away now. I really, really hope you try to stop me."

"You are tough when you can ambush, aren't you? Does that gun make you feel strong? You are such a little punk."

"Does Agent Bitch need another beating to calm her nerves? Please do not feel left out; soon, I will come for you, and when I do, I will kill you very slowly and enjoy every minute."

"Did you kill Dr. Millstead slowly, like a sick freak?"

"No American Bitch, I killed her with one perfect blow to her throat, and she died instantly. She was so frail."

"You probably needed Chen's help to kill her."

"Now, do not be silly. I killed her all by myself, but my friend Chen here did help me dispose of the body. We are a good team."

"You're a coward and a sick, perverted Asian whore."

Jun stretches her right arm to swing a backhand across Diane's mouth, but the agent is prepared and catches her wrist and, with one fluid motion, removes her Glock from under the blanket and presses it into Jun Li's temple.

"You got what you need, Brad?" she yells.

At the signal, Roger rushes from the bathroom and pins Chen Zhao to the wall, relieving him of his weapon. The second 'patient' sits up in bed, focusing a revolver on both mercenaries.

Brad rushes through the door on cue with the uniformed officers close behind, and they secure the scene.

Pamela sits quietly and exhales a huge sigh of relief.

"DC Police, you are both under arrest. Boy, does that feel good," yells Detective Jones. The officers disarm and cuff the would-be kidnappers. Brad forces both perps face down onto one of the beds.

Diane adds insult to injury, "I hope you enjoy the next thirty years in a cell, bitch."

"What do you think you are charging us with, officer? We did not break any laws?"

"Oh, let me see," Brad snickers, "would you like to hear it in your own words?"

Diane picks up the recorder and plays the tape.

"No, American Bitch, I killed her with one perfect blow to her throat. She died instantly. She was so frail."

"Thank you for the confession. Your fate is sealed, Jun Li. And thank you for implicating your partner as an accomplice."

Brad and the four uniformed officers begin to escort the pair out of the room and down the hall. Candace dresses quickly to join them. She thanks Diane for including her before she scurries from the room.

Vitullo starts to don her clothes with Roger there to assist her. She hangs her jacket over her shoulder.

"Thanks for being there, partner."

"Like I told you before, I would walk through hell for you, but a bathroom?" Both agents mustered a smile. With the tension eased, they can afford to relax for a moment.

The team leaves the scene and makes its way down to the lobby. Diane hugs Pamela. "You're a brave girl."

"Detective Jones, this is your collar, but tell your CO this is an ongoing NSA operation. No bail, no phone calls, and no visitors for forty-eight hours. Got it?"

"Got it, Agent Vitullo. It was a real pleasure working on an operation with you. I need to get to the precinct and deal with all this paperwork. Sorry, I cannot drive you back to the house."

"Don't worry, the three of us can Uber."

From the far side of the lobby, they hear, "Do not be silly, Diane. I am off in fifteen minutes. I will be happy to drive you three back."

She turns to see a smiling and relieved Dr. Parisi standing arms crossed.

"Doctor Dreamy to the rescue? Seriously, I do want to thank you again for helping us out today. Two violent psychopaths are now off the street, thanks to you."

"I am so grateful you're okay, Diane Vitullo."

Dr. Will tells them to wait just two minutes as he rushes to his office to grab his keys and lock the door.

Ten minutes later they are walking into the parking lot toward a shiny new BMW 750. "Get in, crew. I will have you there in no time."

As promised, the smooth ride seems way too short as the sedan pulls into Detective Jones's driveway. Roger and Pam exited the vehicle and headed into the house. Diane lags back to thank the doctor for everything he did today.

"I'd love to invite you inside, but we have quite the crowd bunking here."

"I understand, but I am so glad I gave you my card. I was so hoping to see you again."

Diane reaches into her jacket and pulls out her card.

"Now that you know who I really am, I think it is only fair you should have my card as well."

She extends her hand toward him; he takes both card and hand and pulls it gently toward him. Both bodies lean into one another, and their lips meet. A long, hot, steamy kiss ensues. Diane does not know how many minutes elapse in his embrace. She is lost in the moment. When they notice the blinds move in the front window, they both sit back, a bit embarrassed.

"I hope you don't mind if I use this card real soon."

An elated Diane responds, "I'm sort of counting on it."

She exits the car and walks into the house, never feeling the pavement under her feet.

Chapter 34

Saturday 9:00 PM, Jones Residence, 4th Pl. SW, Washington, DC

Brad calls from the precinct, delighted to have been given full credit for the collar. It will serve as a nice highlight in his next performance review.

He offers to purchase an array of pizzas and pick them up on his way home if the group agrees. He then asks Roger to check the beer and wine reserves. Roger gives him a thumbs up on both. The ensemble agrees that pizza would be a welcome dinner item.

Diane likes the thought. "Okay, we will have a nice celebration, but then we will get back to work. This could be an all-night session. I want enough ammunition to send shivers down ParTec Industries' collective spine on Monday." Everyone is in total agreement, none more so than Pamela, whose joy is tempered by her deep concerns and feelings for Dr. Allen.

Thirty minutes after the phone call, Brad returns to the house with a stack of piping hot pies. The famished quartet gorges themselves on tomato sauce, cheese, sausage, and pepperoni. Several bottles of wine are uncorked, and several beers are uncapped. The well-earned celebration provides a terrific release from the earlier tensions of the day.

The group cheers Diane and her masterful plan to gain a confession out of the foreign killers.

She graciously acknowledges their praise but also is careful to point out that without their assistance, none of it would have happened. She also states that they cannot lose sight of the ultimate prize. They need to find Dr. Allen and deal with the anomaly. She makes eye contact with Pam, understanding a little more about those feelings now than she did before her trip to the emergency room. She also thanks Brad for his limitless assistance, both professionally and personally. Finally, she salutes Agent Roger Edwards, her rock and her confidant.

The merriment continues until 11:15 PM, when the mood changes. Spent pizza boxes are cleared. Empty bottles are trashed. Still upbeat, the team begins focusing on their next target, ParTec Industries.

"Okay, let's see where we are," says Diane.

Sensing her urgency to assist, she requests Pam begin the reporting with her profile on Gunther Dryden.

<u>Gunther Dryden</u>

Born: 1962   Died: 2019

Columbus, Ohio
Grandview Heights High School, Class of 1980
University of Pittsburgh, Class of 1984
Bachelor's degree in accounting
Average student
Two years of varsity football / two years of varsity soccer.
Married in 1988 Spouse. Unknown
Children: Daniel, born 1990 / Kristen, born 1992
Work: Employed by Impulse Trucking 1989 (in-laws business)
Founded ParTec Industries 2008
Cause of death: Automobile accident with wife.

Diane praises Pam's thoroughness but requests she obtain the maiden name of Gunther's spouse.

Colonel Marshal Fielding

Born: 1964   Died:

Columbus Ohio
Grandview Heights High School Class of 1982
US Military Academy West Point Class of 1986
Bachelor's degree in supply chain/deployment
A + Student
No sports listed.
Single, never married.
Children: None
Work: Employed by the United States Army
        Fort Benning, GA 1986 -1990
        Operation Desert Storm 1991- 1996 Resupply
        Camp Buehring, Kuwait 1997-2000
        Pentagon 2000-2004
        Iraq II-2004 -2010
        Pentagon 2011 -2024

"Thank you, Roger. So, Gunther and the Colonel most probably knew each other. Growing up in the same town and attending the same high school for at least two years together. There is at least circumstantial evidence of a relationship. Not rock-solid proof, but a nexus is a good place to start."

Diane begins to write this on the whiteboard when Pam stands up, screaming, "Holy cow, you're not going to believe this."

All eyes point to her as she blurts out, "Gunther Dryden was married to Marsha Fielding, the Colonel's younger sister."

Roger looks at Diane, and both know they now have at least one arrow in their quiver for Monday's chat.

"Great job, Pamela. Ever think about joining the NSA?"

"Thank you, Diane, but NO, THANK YOU."

"Okay. Brad, you're up. What can you tell us about ParTec Industries?"

Brad stands and walks to the whiteboard.

"Let's start with the building. I have a few contacts in the Fire Chief's office. ParTec bought the property ten years ago. The transaction was in cash. The building is in decent shape, and there are no outstanding violations. It is listed in the office/warehouse category, and there are no manufacturing facilities on the premises. The top floor is divided between a boardroom and residential space, which I assume is for the two owners. The third floor is for office use. The first two floors are used solely as warehouse space."

"This alone is not very enlightening. However, when you combine it with what Roger has been able to charm out of his military buddies, we are left with quite the puzzle."

"Over the last ten years, Partec Industries has bid on six projects per year. A consistent number every year. Six and only six projects. Coincidently, of the six, they have won three and lost three each year without exception. The bids they have won range from $6 million to $8 million each. The steadiness is mind-boggling. The wins are all legitimate. The GSA records show they were the low bidder for as many of them as we could find. If you look at any given year, nothing stands out, but taken as a whole is quite astonishing."

Roger interjects. "We think the three losing bids are decoys designed to legitimize the winning ones."

"That makes a lot of sense and is quite clever, but if they are the bona fide low bid, how are they doing it, and how much money are they raking in?" asks Diane.

"I have a degree in accounting, not mind reading, so for me to figure that out, I will need to get into their books and see what the acquisition costs were for the materials sold. The difference would equal their profit."

"So, what is their secret?" ponders Diane.

"Well, we did learn that the firm of Howard P. Small, PC, handles all their books. Their office is at 6894 Old Dominion Drive. And get this: he wasn't born in Columbus, OH but he did go to the University of Pittsburgh at the same time as Gunther. Can you get us a warrant, Diane?" asks Detective Jones.

"Not exactly, but tomorrow is Sunday, and Roger picks a mean lock."

"You okay with a little breaking and entering, cupcake?" snickers agent Edwards.

Brad smirks back, "I wouldn't miss it for the world."

"Alright, let's all get a good night's sleep. We got some work to do in the morning."

Diane pulls Roger aside. "We better take Pamela with us. I can't risk leaving her alone."

Roger concurs. Then, he grabs Diane's arm. "This case reeks like a dead fish partner. Something is rotten to the core here. I don't like the vibes I'm getting."

"I wish I could disagree, partner. I so wish I could."

Chapter 35

Sunday 9:00 AM, Offices of Howard P. Small PC., 6894 Old Dominion Drive, McLean, VA

Detective Jones parks his car one block east of the target and the four would be perps travel the rest on foot. They move stealthily along the sidewalk, each wearing gray hoodies to shield them from any video cameras. When they reach the building, numbered 6894, they push the door, checking to see if it is locked. When it swings open freely, they duck quickly inside. A quick scan reveals the absence of any security personnel. They arrive at the desired suite in seconds.

It is situated towards the rear of the building and somewhat obscured. Perfect conditions for a break-in. The lock is simple, and Roger's nimble fingers solve it in no time. On first observation, it appears that Mr. Small's name is indicative of his client list. There are only two desks inside and two large vertical filing cabinets. ParTec Industries occupies at least 80% of the available space. There are a couple of files listed in other names, but they are dominated by the company in question. Brad Jones is the only one in the group with any advanced accounting knowledge, so he takes the lead.

He begins by inspecting last year's files and looking for IRS returns, income statements, and balance sheets. His portable scanner is working overtime, recording anything he feels might be pertinent. When complete, he moves on to the prior year and repeats the process. This continues until they reach back a decade. The further back Brad goes, the more puzzled he appears. He shakes his head and continues to scan. The salient information is preserved, and useless information is discarded.

At the ninety-minute mark, Rogers calls out from across the office, "Hey, cupcake, how much longer? We don't have all day."

"Scanning the last document now."

"Great, this place is filthy."

Diane had passed the time trying to get some information on Mr. Small himself. A diploma on the wall reveals he attended the University of Pittsburgh on or about the same time as Gunther Dryden. Some photographs appear to show him on campus. She makes a mental note and moves on, looking for additional clues. Two bottles of vodka in the top drawer paint a less-than-rosy picture of the current state of his life.

When the last document is scanned, they re-don their hoodies and slowly filter out of the suite. Upon arriving back at the car, Agent Edwards can no longer contain his curiosity.

"Well, do you have anything?"

Brad presses the ignition. "You're not going to believe what I just saw, but I'll need some time to lay it all out."

The ride back to Fourth Place begins, and Diane suggests they stop at the Safeway to pick up some breakfast supplies. She wasn't the most talented chef, but her head needed to be cleared, and cooking a nice meal would work just fine. She could always work up a good omelet when pressed.

They reach the garage and begin unpacking.

"Roger, if you don't mind helping Brad finish his report, I'll go prepare breakfast. Pam, do you mind assisting?"

Pam readily accepts the invitation to contribute.

The girls enter the kitchen, tossing pans on the stove, and begin cracking some eggs. Brad and Roger move to the desk and start painting a financial picture of ParTec Industries. In forty-five minutes, all were seated around the table, diving into a cheese and onion omelet, bacon, and home fries. Brad devours his entire meal without speaking a word. When all the food has been consumed, the group returns to its makeshift conference center, leaving all the plates as they lie.

"Detective Jones, you have us all in suspense. We need your thoughts now," orders Diane.

Brad clears his throat, "Here goes. We went back ten years and reviewed income statements, balance sheets, and IRS filings. Over that time frame, ParTec has won thirty GSA bids for military equipment, ranging from rifles to rocket launchers and hand grenades to Humvees. The sum of those bids is just under $250 million dollars. But that's not the amazing part. In those ten years, I could not find a single dollar spent to acquire any of those assets."

The room goes completely silent.

Roger speaks first, "It's easy to underbid when you're getting the product for free."

The reality of what has occurred hits Diane like a tidal wave. "All this time, the scrutiny has always been placed on the bidding process. It's freaking genius. The bids are legit. The acquisitions are compromised."

Roger adds, "How brilliant is that? And who do they know to be able to work through that?"

"It's got to be someone high in the Pentagon. How else could they hide this, and how do they know what to supply? We need to rattle some cages tomorrow, Roger, and see what shakes out."

Agent Edwards, "That's exactly what I am afraid of."

Diane replies, "What do they say about omelets and eggs."

Brad adds, "There's something else that's a bit unusual. It appears that when comparing the balance sheets with the income statements, almost half the earned profits have been removed from the company."

"What do you make of that, Brad?" questions Diane.

"My guess is that it has been transferred to offshore accounts in the event a quick getaway is necessary. A sort of illegal golden parachute for the fleeing executive."

"I am going to check back in with Myles. He needs to start taking this seriously."

Pamela volunteers to do cleanup duty, and Roger offers to assist. Brad's trash can does now resemble that of a frat house, but the home is rendered spotless.

Chapter 36
Sunday 2:00 PM, NSA Headquarters, Undisclosed location, Chicago, IL

Diane hesitates as she stares at the phone. She knows this call must be made but she can't decide on how much information to reveal. She was positive that Myles was a good man and loyal to the agency, but he was a rules follower. And following rules meant filling out reports. Reports she didn't want it published just yet. It was apparent they were dealing with a whale. Someone with the resources to get ParTec this kind of equipment at no cost was powerful. We are talking about high-level Pentagon power. Possibly as high as a member of the Joint Chiefs. Whoever it was she was certain they had the ability to crush her and any investigation if they were warned. This was a delicate matter, and caution was necessary. She would only reveal what she absolutely had to. The call is placed.

"Agent Vitello, glad to hear from you so soon."

"Sir, I wanted to update you on our findings and our suspicions before our visit to ParTec tomorrow."

"Proceed, Vitullo. We did some checking, but they seem clean. Bids all seemed clean."

"We had done the same research, sir and agreed from the back end everything was kosher. However, we found some inconsistencies on the procurement side. I need to do some more work to clear up our hypothesis. We also made some connections between Gunther Dryden and Colonel Fielding. Seems that Dryden married Fielding's sister."

"Interesting, agent, you got my attention."

"We don't know the mechanics of the scheme yet, sir, but we are close. According to our investigation, they made approximately $250 million on government contracts in the last ten years."

"Did you say $250 million?"

"Yes, sir. We looked at their books in an unauthorized way. I kept my promise, no warrants. Their accountant had college ties to Dryden. We can't use what we found in court, but it will aid the overall investigation."

"Ah, good, Vitullo, you do have ears, but say no more. Don't compromise me."

"I won't, sir. Tomorrow, we will have a much better fix on that company and their owners."

"Good, keep me posted. That all, Agent?

"Sir, I do have one more request. I know Director Wilson recently passed away from a heart attack, I believe."

"Where are you going with this, Diane?"

"Is the scene still preserved?"

"Yes, deaths of all high-level officials are treated as crime scenes until we are certain otherwise."

"Great, sir, could you dust his insulin bottles for me?"

"What are we getting to here, Vitullo? You can't be serious."

"Well, sir, he may have been the one helping ParTec, and Dryden or Fielding may have panicked under the heat."

"I will honor your request, agent, but the Director was the cleanest person in DC. He squeaked."

"I understand it's just that the term of his directorship coincides exactly with the rise of ParTec. He was promoted from Deputy Director to Director exactly ten years ago. It could be a coincidence, but we need to rule it out, sir."

"I hate my job, Agent, and you are correct. We need to rule it out. I'll dust them for you. If there's nothing else, I will wait for your next call. Stay safe."

"I intend to, sir."

Chapter 37

Monday 10:00 AM, Penthouse ParTec Industries, Old Dominion Drive & Lowell Ave., McLean, VA

Seated in the front seat of Detective Jones's sedan, Diane and Roger stared at each other. They were parked in the garage on Old Dominion Drive at the corner of Lowell Avenue. The offices of ParTec Industries loomed over them. The next hour would be critical to the success of their investigation. They needed to create a ripple but not start a wave. The savvy veterans knew how vital tone and dialogue were to the interview process. They silently hoped their late-night rehearsal was enough to prepare them for the task at hand. Ideally, isolated interviews would have been sought. They would unquestionably reveal more. Unfortunately, the agents doubted the siblings would agree to speak under those terms. A debate had arisen about whether to call ahead for an appointment. They ultimately decided the element of surprise would better serve their needs.

"It's now or never, partner."

"Let's move."

The walk to the elevator seemed to take forever as each agent mulled the critical agenda in their mind. Diane and Roger were a great team. They acted harmoniously and, at times, could read each other's thoughts. They would need that synchronicity today.

The offices were located on the third floor of the four-story structure. Reaching the top floor was today's first goal.

Three is pressed on the panel before them, and the cage slowly rises, opening to a reception area. The pair discretely approaches the young woman seated at the desk behind a large monitor. They remove their wallets to show her their badges while handing her two business cards.

Diane opens, "Agent Vitullo and Agent Edwards, National Security Agency. We are here to see Daniel and Kristen Dryden on a sensitive but urgent matter."

"Do you have an appointment?"

"No, but we would appreciate if you notify them of our presence due to the urgency."

The flustered clerk nearly drops the phone, trying to accept the cards and call upstairs all at once. The agents backed away from the desk, allowing her to speak freely into the mouthpiece. The call ends, and the girl glances up at Diane.

"Agents, could you please have a seat over there and make yourselves comfortable? The Drydens can see you in fifteen minutes. Can I get you something to drink, coffee or tea?

The offer is politely declined.

The fifteen minutes linger to nearly thirty before the receptionist walks over and offers to escort them to the penthouse. They return to the elevator lobby but are directed to a smaller set of doors.

"This is the elevator for the boardroom and residence, agents. Someone will greet you upstairs."

She reaches in and presses the button quickly, retrieving her arm before the door shuts.

Worried they are being monitored, the agents remain quiet. They prepare themselves for any unexpected activity when the doors open. To be safe, Diane reaches for her holster under her jacket.

The elevator stops on the fourth floor, and they are greeted by one of the servants who is offering to lead them into the residence.

"The Dryden's would like you to join them for breakfast. Follow me, please."

The walk from the boardroom to the residence is short, and they follow the servant into the dining room. Seated at the head of the table is Daniel, dressed in his normal navy blue blazer and khaki trousers. Kristen sits to his right and wears a plain black pantsuit.

Daniel assumes control immediately.

"Sit down, agents, and please feel free to order anything you desire. My chef is the best on the Beltway."

Diane counters, "Thank you for the gracious offer but it is not our desire to impose. Coffee will be fine."

His reply is polite but curt. "Well, agents, you must do this enough to realize that just flashing those badges can create a certain level of imposition."

"Touche, Daniel, I guess I do realize that, and sometimes I count on it, but we come here today as information gatherers, not inquisitors."

"Well parried, agent... Vitullo, is it?"

"Thank you, Mr. Dryden."

"Please call me Daniel and my sister Kristen. Why don't we leave the formalities to the inquisitors?"

"Agreed."

Rogers's impeccable timing allows him to jump in and alter the pace of the conversation.

"Daniel, Kristen, I am sure you are curious as to why we are here?"

Kristen responds, "I was hoping it was for the eggs benedict." The remark is followed by laughter.

When it subsides, Roger counters, "No, we are here investigating a murder."

The first ripple spreads through the conversation.

"Please go on," stammers a befuddled CEO.

The agents see the first chink in the siblings' smug armor.

"A scientist named Stephanie Millstead was murdered minutes from her house in Warrenville, IL."

"Well, I don't think we can help you, agent. My sister and I have never even been to Illinois."

Diane reaches into her case while Roger maintains control of the floor.

"On the contrary, we believe you can."

As the final word of Rogers's sentence leaves his mouth, Diane places two photographs exactly as choreographed squarely under the faces of both Drydens. Kristen shows no reaction, but Daniel's face betrays him for several long seconds before he can restore his composure.

A shared glance between the agents signals the mutual understanding they have uncovered chink number two.

Diane interjects, "Their names are Chen Zhao and Jun Li."

Her words are followed by silence. Rogers pauses, allowing the moment to settle in, then follows with, "We believe they are mercenaries selling their services to the highest bidder."

A now clearly unnerved Daniel inquires, "Why would you question us about Chinese mercenaries and a murder in Chicago."

Chink numbers three and four.

Diane rapidly responds, "Well, how astute you are, Daniel. They are indeed Chinese, and for not ever being in Illinois, you seem to know its geography pretty well."

A bead of sweat now runs down Daniel's furrowed brow. Control has now shifted to the two agents.

In a valiant effort to save her brother, Kristen interjects some humor, hoping the delay will allow him to regroup.

"Must be the kung pao chicken we ate for dinner last night."

A stern Edwards presses the advantage. "No, actually, we are here because we have reports of them being in this immediate area. We were wondering whether they were employed here and, if so, to advise you of the potential danger."

"Well, I... uhh... I can forward the photographs to our Human Resources people and see if they recognize either. Unfortunately, she is out sick today. Can we keep the photos until she returns?"

"Certainly, Daniel, we have plenty. Would you like another copy?"

Before he can answer, Roger pressures, "How many people work in this building?"

Kristen needs to alter the conversation. "Agents, excuse my interruption, but this sounds a lot like an inquisition to me."

"On the contrary, I am an admirer of efficiency. I noticed that you seem to maintain a lean workforce. With an annual gross revenue of approximately $15 million dollars, you must be rolling in cash. A tip of my hat to you."

Daniel's shirt is now dripping with perspiration, and he's beginning to lose control of his nervous tick. His jacket hides the dark blue patches under his arms, and a sinking feeling engulfs him.

"There are lots of expenses beyond employees, Agent Edwards. We wish we were as efficient as you perceive."

"I guess a pair of Chinese mercenaries would set the miscellaneous expense budget back quite a bit."

Desperate to salvage some repose, Kristen responds while Daniel stutters. "They certainly would, Agent Edwards. Are Korean mercenaries any cheaper?"

Roger stares at Kristen while she tries to bail her brother out of a jam.

Diane says, "That's another question for the HR team, Kristen. Do you have anything else, Roger?"

"No, Diane, I believe that is everything. We thank you so much for your time."

Diane offers, "Is there anything you want to ask us before we leave?"

"No, Agent Vitullo, we will have our Human Resources Manager contact the number on your card."

Both agents rise and extend their hands outward to shake those of their hosts prior to turning toward the exit. After taking four calculated steps, Diane stops and then turns. Doing her best to look forgetful, she speaks, "I am so sorry. May I impose on you for one more question?"

"Certainly."

"Your company deals with the military. Am I correct?"

"Yes, agent, we do."

"Have you ever encountered a Colonel Marshall Fielding in your dealings?"

Kristen answers, trying to avoid the trap, "Well, that's two questions now, right agent?"

Unfortunately for him, Daniel takes the bait. "I don't believe we recognize that name. Why are you asking?"

"You caught me red-handed, Kristen. It was. He was Dr. Millstead's supervisor in Illinois. That's all."

The agents remain mum on the elevator down to level 1, resisting the urge to high-five until they are out of view of any potential cameras. However, an automatic camera clicks on the license plate of their vehicle as it exits the garage.

Upstairs, the siblings are in full-blown damage control. Daniel is trembling on the verge of a nervous breakdown. His condition deteriorates rapidly. The pressures are overwhelming his capacity to cope. Kristen rushes to the medical cabinet and, with a syringe, administers a high dosage of a strong tranquilizer. In minutes, her beleaguered CEO and brother are resting comfortably.

Once Daniel falls into his slumber, his sister closes the bedroom door and marches to the terminal. Direct action is needed. She types in the necessary code to reach the entity known only as Ice.

YOU WERE WISE TO CONTACT ME, DEAR KRISTEN.

THE SITUATION REQUIRES IMMEDIATE AND DRASTIC ACTION. YOU HAVE PERFORMED WELL IN THE PAST. ARE YOU PREPARED TO TAKE THE NEXT STEPS?

I AM ALWAYS YOUR LOYAL AND FAITHFUL SERVANT. I HAVE DONE ALL THAT WAS ASKED FOR WITHOUT QUESTION.

YES, YOU HAVE MY DEAR ON AT LEAST ON TWO PREVIOUS OCCASIONS. I KNEW WHEN YOU WERE A CHILD THAT YOU WERE SPECIAL. YOU HAVE PROVEN THAT IN THE YEARS SINCE. IT HAS NOT GONE WITHOUT NOTICE OR MERIT. WHEN I NEEDED SOMEONE, I COULD ALWAYS COUNT ON YOU. YOU HAVE ONE FINAL DUTY TO CLEAN UP DANIEL'S MESS THEN YOU WILL BE REWARDED BEYOND YOUR WILDEST IMAGINATION. HERE IS WHAT NEEDS TO BE DONE.

Kristen reads the new orders given in the sequence of occurrence, making careful notes to ensure precision.

IT WILL BE DONE AS REQUESTED, SIR.

MY PRECIOUS, YOU ARE VERY SPECIAL TO ME. TAKE EXTRA CARE TO MAKE CERTAIN EVERYTHING IS DONE EXACTLY AS I HAVE LAID OUT.

AND DANIEL, SIR? YOU HAVEN'T GIVEN ME ANY INSTRUCTIONS ON HOW TO DEAL WITH HIM.

I THINK YOU KNOW WHAT MUST BE DONE. THIS WORLD IS NOT FOR THE WEAK. CAN YOU HANDLE THAT TASK?

YES, SIR, IT WILL BE HANDLED AS YOU WISH.

Chapter 38

Monday 5:00 PM, Safe House, Scotts Run Rd., McLean, VA

Doctor Allen sat across from his sister-in-law, careful not to engage in any conversation that would betray their secret. He was frustrated and tired of being the victim. Through a series of facial gestures and signals, he tried to make Ursula aware of his intention to act. Her instincts helped her to realize something was imminent, but when and how were still unknown.

Frustration was also mounting on the other side as the "jailer" had been awaiting the arrival of the correct hostage for nearly two days now. Time was running out. The smooth plan they had orchestrated was falling apart bit by bit. The Asian mercenaries had vanished, throwing a wrench in the recovery operation. He dials his phone, reaching out to his associate. Someone needs to contact ParTec Industries and get some guidance on the next move before panic and chaos take control. His partner answers the phone. Kristen has been in contact. There is a new plan. He will return shortly to fill him in and assist in the implementation.

Cameron sensed that the situation would soon change and decided to strike now. The known is always better than the unknown. Dinner time was approaching, and they wouldn't get another chance.

When the preoccupied man in the ski mask enters with a tray of food, Cam inches to the far side of the room. He motions for Ursula to do the same on the opposite side. Only one captive can be visible, given the space and the mask limiting his peripheral vision. A plate is lifted from the tray and offered first to the female captive. His back is turned to Cam, so he strikes, sending a chair to the base of the man's skull. The blow drops him to both knees. He looks behind him, trying to comprehend what just happened, allowing Ursula to finish the job by cracking a porcelain plate over his skull. The man lies sprawled between them. Ursula grabs a knife from the dinner tray and slides it into her jeans. They quickly search his pockets and find the keys.

Precious minutes are wasted as, by trial and error, they located the correct key. He frees himself, then his sister-in-law, and locks the captor in her place. Once the chain is secured around his legs, they make their way out of one room and into the next. Freedom lies just beyond the front door. He grabs Ursula by the hands and opens it, anticipating his first encounter with the sun in several long days. What he gets is the barrel of a pistol pointed directly at his forehead. His captor's companion has returned to share the new orders just in time to thwart his escape.

"Doc, if you weren't so valuable, I would dish out a world of pain on your ass and make you pay for this."

His partner is freed, and the rightful captives are returned to their places. The duo then prepares to execute their new plan: to get the van ready. They have been told to move out in a few hours.

Chapter 39

Monday 10:00 PM, Fermi Lab., Batavia, IL

Colonel Fielding was lying in bed in his makeshift apartment inside Fermi Lab. Forced to provide twenty-four-hour security, he thought it best to create a residence to maximize his comfort level. Lying next to him was the naked body of Sergeant Ann Kelly. Both torsos were dripping with sweat caused by a recently completed carnal. Fielding's warped mind mused to himself, "Maybe I'll take this bitch with me after all." Never one to extoll the virtues of a woman, he lies selfishly, weighing the difference between the lure of exotic teens versus the familiar and reliable. His once-promising military mind has degenerated into a demented ego-centric vessel.

As he ponders the days of promise to come, he hears his phone stowed on the nightstand begin to buzz. Looking over, the name *Kristen Dryden* flashes in the dial. Never a fan of the Drydens, he mumbles to himself, "It's after ten. This better be good." He answers the call in his usual gruff manner.

Kristen is all business, starting abruptly with, "Tell your whore to go fetch a glass of water. This is important."

His face reddens, but he motions for the sergeant to go make two more drinks.

Kristen was the youngest daughter of Gunther and his sister Marsha. The family never understood what she saw in that loser. They had to support both almost from the day their honeymoon ended. It wasn't until years later, through a quirk of fate, that Gunther reunited with an old navy buddy. He started a company and then moved to the DC area. Slowly, it became profitable. After a while, they contacted the Colonel to work with them, and the money began to flow. Still, the genius lay with Gunther's mysterious friend. His concept was cunning and spectacular. None of them could figure out how it was done.

The money poured in, and his family didn't ask any questions. When Gunther and Marsha were killed in the accident five years ago, Daniel took over the reins. He was the kind of prissy boy you wanted to take out to the woodshed. Fielding never thought he was very bright or deserving, but after all, they didn't need a rocket scientist. They relied on the mystery man, and profits kept rising. Everything was great until that fateful night here at the lab. Things haven't been smooth since. He was forced to relocate here to babysit a bunch of geeky scientists in their white lab coats. The only thing that kept him going was the goal of unprecedented wealth and Mai Tais on the beach.

"Okay, Kristen, she is gone. What's on your mind this evening."

"There has been a change in plans, Colonel. He wants to accelerate our timetable. I am using my jet to fly all the appropriate people necessary for this thing to happen tomorrow night. Arrange for the lab to be empty save for you, Salazar, and the bimbo. Two of my security people will accompany the six prisoners on the flight and stay with you. The girl will be present, and Allen will cooperate. Once we have the required amount of material, shut everything down

193

and eliminate everyone, including Salazar. No loose ends. Got it?"

"So, everyone that is brought will be terminated?"

"What is it about no loose ends that confuse you, Colonel?"

"Even your security people?"

"Yes"

"You are the only one that walks out of that building alive with the material and or the correct flash drive. Find a way to make that work. We will send a helicopter to fly you to the extraction point."

"Yes, Kristen, I understand completely. Good night."

Sergeant Kelly returns with two large Jack and Cokes, and the Colonel grins. "Now, where were we?"

Might as well get one more ride on that beautiful body while I can. Looks like fate has dictated our futures.

Chapter 40

Tuesday 12:00 AM, Penthouse ParTec Industries, Old Dominion Drive & Lowell Ave, McLean, VA

The coup was complete. The entire operation now relied on Kristen. Her brother had finally been exposed as the inept poser he was. This was her chance to lead. All those years she did all the dirty work, and he got all the credit. This was her time to shine. The "man" was now reliant on her, and she would make everything come together.

The interview this morning was designed for one purpose. The agents were looking for the weak link. They found it and nearly broke it. But once again, Kristen saved the day. First, the message to "Ice" to alert him, and second, the bullet placed in her brother's skull. He was too weak to live.

This was now her plan, and she would make certain it succeeded. The best lure was to offer something the prey was looking for. Her next call would do exactly that. The agents were good, and she needed a way to lower their guard. A deep breath is taken as she rehearses for her Oscar moment. She had to sound sincere. It would be the key ingredient to set everything in motion. Kristen stared at the card in her hand as she dialed the number. There would be no turning back. It was now or never.

A groggy voice answers at the other end.

"This is Agent Vitullo. How can I help you?"

"Agent, this is Kristen Dryden. Please help me—I am afraid for my life."

"Calm down, tell me what's happening."

"My brother has snapped; he's gone mad, ranting and raving. Your visit here has caused him to lose control. I do not know what kind of business he was doing, but you scared him. He has a gun and is waving it around the apartment. I'm locked in my bedroom. I am too frightened to leave. He's going to kill someone or himself. I need your help."

"Stay in your bedroom. Keep the door locked and barricade it if you can. We will be right there."

"Please hurry. I'm so scared."

"Stay on the line. You need to turn off the alarm and unlock the elevators. We are on our way."

Diane slides into a pair of jeans and a pullover. Searching for shoes, she knocks on Roger's door.

"Get up, Daniel Dryden has snapped. His sister needs our help."

They rush down to the garage grabbing the keys and leaving a note for its owner on the way. Hopping into Brad's car, they sped off, headed toward Mclean, VA.

But the agents are only half of her problem. For her to claim success, one more critical step needed to be taken. She silently hopes that this one carefully orchestrated phone call can set both in motion.

Fortunately, earlier today, they were able to ascertain Detective Jones's address from the license plate of his car. A van was sent to stake out the house and wait for the agent's departure. Once left unguarded, the girls' apprehension would be simple. They would take the detective as well to eliminate another loose end. When the agent's car turns off the street, the van's engine ignites, and it inches its way to the correct number. Two armed men exit and force their way into the residence. One heads to the Detective's bedroom and holds him at gunpoint. The other wrestles the girl from her blanket and drags her into the living room. Both are gagged and bound before being led outside into the waiting van. The stunned prisoners are thrown in the back, left to wonder what had just happened.

Meanwhile, the NSA agents sped along the George Washington Memorial Parkway, and nineteen minutes later, they boarded the public elevator on Old Dominion Parkway, prepared to rescue the younger Dryden from her deranged brother. They exit the main lift and board the one exclusive to the fourth floor. It seems like days before the doors open to reveal the expanse of the dimly lit boardroom. The phone call made mention of the apartment, but a quick search of the business portion was necessary to ensure it was secure before they ventured further inward. When cleared, the duo proceeded across the hall. There was an eerie silence as the silhouettes of Kristen and Daniel appeared seated in the same dining room chairs they occupied this morning. Diane led the way forward while Roger covered her back.

"Kristen, are you ok?"

As Diane nears, she sees what looks like blood on Kristen's blouse.

"Are you hurt?"

"No, Agent Vitullo. I am fine."

Only when she is directly over the table, does she see the gaping wound in Daniel's head.

"What happened?"

"I don't know; I heard a gunshot and left the bedroom to see what happened, and he was sitting here."

"Did he try to harm you?"

"No, he was dead by the time I reached the table. Detective, please help me. I am so frightened."

Diane feels his neck for a pulse, but the body is colder than it should be. Something is wrong. At that very moment, two ParTec security agents leaped from the shadows and hit Roger with taser strikes. Her partner is shaking violently, and his weapon drops to the floor. Diane turns, giving Kristen the only edge she needs. She rises from the chair and sends her right foot kicking to the back of Diane's head. The attack knocks the gun out of her hands and drops her to the floor. The agent never sees the blow coming and now lies face down in a puddle of her own drool. Kristen stands over her, ready to send another kick into her foe's neck, but realizes that won't be necessary. She smirks at how easily these "professionals" were duped.

When she sees no evidence of a struggle, she leans over, grabs both arms of the unconscious agent, and cuffs her wrists together. Vitullo's limp torso is dragged by her long legs across the floor to where her partner lies. Both are cuffed and gagged.

The buzzing of Kristen's cell phone informs her that the first mission at Brad's house was successful. The van with its two hostages is on the way. She smiles, knowing that the right person is finally in charge. Orders are given to transport all four passengers to a designated location. Her chief security officer accompanies them. She has one more mission, which is to destroy all traces of ParTec Industries. It is the last loose end to handle. She begins to pour the gasoline around the apartment and office, aided by her two employees. When everything is finished, a fire is started, and her two accomplices are eliminated with single bullets to each of their heads.

By the time Kristen makes her triumphant exit from the garage in her shiny white Mercedes, the sun is rising in the morning sky.

Chapter 41

Tuesday 10:00 AM, Ronald Reagan International Airport, Washington, DC

The Gulfstream 650, titled to ParTec Industries, is parked on the tarmac adjacent to the private building managed by Signature DCA. The pilot and co-pilot have been given permission to leave the plane and get a warm breakfast. Departure time is still uncertain.

Several minutes later, a van pulls alongside the parked jet and stops. A fuel truck is requested and makes its way to the front of the plane, obscuring the van from the terminal window. Everything appears to be falling into place. Four bound bodies are roughly yanked out of the van and marched up the stairway and into the fuselage. Agent Vitullo is manhandled into a seat in the rear of the plane and buckled into it. Her shoes are thrown in after her.

Agent Edwards, still stunned by the electricity that invaded his body, is dragged and seated further forward. The third body to be seated is none other than Detective Brad Jones. He gazes out the window in utter disbelief, feeling like a two-bit actor in a cheap spy movie. The last person to emerge from the van is the elusive Pamela Ward. Finally, in their control, they take extreme caution not to injure her. She is carefully led onto the plane and seated. Her role will be a critical one. The van then pulls away, leaving everyone to sit and ponder the current situation. One of the guards remains to keep watch.

There is no movement or conversation for thirty minutes until the next van makes its way to the same location as its predecessor. Doors are opened, and a blonde woman emerges, led up and into the jet. Finally, the most precious cargo of all is carefully pushed up the steps. Dr. Cameron Allen exits the van. His eyes widen as he scans the interior of the Gulfstream, his sharp mind trying to identify his fellow passengers in case it can aid in their escape. He locates the young detective he perceives to be Agent Vitullo and takes the seat next to her. When empty, the van drives off the runway, leaving the second guard to make the trip to Chicago with the prisoners. He places a call to advise his boss that all are on board and awaiting the pilot's return.

The crew eventually enters the cockpit and begins prepping the luxury craft by running through an extensive checklist. It is almost noon when the plane begins its taxi toward the takeoff point. Not a sole inside has any clue of what to expect when they land.

Chapter 42

Tuesday 1:00 PM, Gulfstream 650, Somewhere over Pennsylvania

The sleek jet reaches altitude, heading west for the state of Illinois. The passengers are quiet, all adjusting to the fact they are prisoners of some ill-intentioned entity. The two security guards are seated in the front of the vessel next to Agent Edwards, whom they perceive as the biggest threat.

This allows Dr. Allen to converse freely with the agent he had spoken to on the telephone days earlier.

"I should have listened to you, Agent Vitullo. Perhaps we could have avoided this mess."

"We can't change the past, Doctor. The question is, what do we do now? Did you have a plan?"

"Well, I thought that if I got inside, there might be a way to deal with the void. I have gone over the calculations time and time again in my mind. But please understand, we don't know what it is. All I am bringing to the table is an educated guess. My theories could be worthless. I also knew that if I had repaired it, my life would have been in jeopardy. None of that mattered if Pamela was safe."

"I understand. Tell me more about your plan to deal with the anomaly."

Doctor Allen gets into some technical explanations that leave Diane's head spinning. However, she learns that the critical timing is between levels seven and ten. That's when the deception begins. His goal was to play a scientific shell game, keeping the observers guessing until he was able to nullify the strange anomaly. But with Pamela's life on the line, it didn't matter. He couldn't go forward with it.

"Listen, Cam," warns Diane, "they do not intend for any of us to live. It doesn't matter whether you cooperate or not. I hope you trust me and understand that."

"I do, agent. I should have trusted you sooner."

"Let me work on planning a way out of there. I will just need a signal from you to time our escape properly. They need to think you are cooperating until the last possible minute. For this to work, we will need to catch them with their guard down. We will more than likely be outnumbered by a good margin, so the element of surprise is crucial."

"Well, if all goes correctly, I will power up to level nine and create some kind of excuse to add more power. If I can get them to agree, I can certainly level the playing field. The noise of the equipment should provide you with notice. Each level will have its own distinctive sound. Just keep a running count and be ready to strike. I'll need their help on the next part, but I am hoping that greed will cloud their judgment. I won't know for certain until I see the extent of their desperation. That will determine how far we go, agent. If they cooperate and my theory is sound, our first problem will be solved. I'll rely on your expertise to handle the second one. I promise to give you any edge I can. Just keep my girl safe."

"So, we will need to move when the machine's power back up to level nine. Thank you, doctor. Right now, your theory is a hell of a lot more than I got."

"No, not then. I'll need to get all the way to level ten. If what I am planning works, that's when it will happen. You will know when to strike."

"Understood, I need to be prepared but not go into action until the critical moment."

"Detective, this is all theory; I cannot guarantee success."

"Neither can I, doctor, neither can I."

Chapter 43

Tuesday 3:00 PM, DuPage Airport, 2700 International Drive, West Chicago, IL

The flight to Illinois was diverted several times since it departed Ronald Reagan International Airport. A line of harsh weather was making its way across the Midwest, creating a turbulent storm front. Several course and altitude corrections were required to minimize its volatility. This resulted in a much longer duration than the planners originally anticipated. When the wheels of the Gulfstream touched down on the runway at DuPage Airport the clock was reading 3:30 PM.

Lying just six miles north of the lab, the small airport rests within a fourteen-minute drive of their ultimate destination. This facility was chosen because of the minimum level of traffic traversing its terminal. The terminal was a fraction of the size of O'Hare. Fewer people made it easier to conceal today's manifest of six unwilling passengers. A large van covered with Radioactive Hazard decals stops next to the plane. The ruse is designed to carefully coordinate with the Colonel's plan to evacuate the lab. Hazmat suits are rushed up the stairway, and each "passenger" is told to wear one, including the two security guards.

One by one, the suited figures disembark and enter the extremely decorated vehicle. They are ordered into position just as they are seated inside the plane. Extra attention was again paid to the burly NSA agent.

Due to the delay, Colonel Fielding needed to postpone the timing of the "accident." This would allow him to prevent the night shift from entering his facility. The adjusted time would be moved until just after 5:00 PM. That should give them a twelve-hour window to complete their task, eliminate the loose ends, and make their escape. For added insurance, he assigned two M.P.s from the Rock Island Arsenal in Moline, IL, to meet the van before it set out on its drive to Batavia. They were Sergeant Thomas May and Corporal Elaine Nichols. The soldiers arrived fully armed and attired in their field camo. Their M.P. armbands were clearly visible. The site of six handcuffed people in Hazmat suits sitting on a plane seemed a bit odd. But they were soldiers, and their job was to get those passengers to Fermi without incident.

The Colonel had advised them to obey the man with the aviator sunglasses as he was directing the mission until they reached their destination. Once at the lab, he would take charge. They were also briefed on the relative threat level of the passengers, resulting in each of them keeping an eye on one of the NSA agents throughout the ride.

Chapter 44

Tuesday 5:00 PM, Fermi Lab. Batavia, IL

At precisely 4:45 PM, the Colonel sounds the alarm. A shrill siren screeches its warning for all to hear. As per the countless practice drills, the employees were instructed to evacuate the building and cue in the parking lot a safe distance away from the structure. Fielding uses every channel at his disposal to warn of a radiation leak and the necessity to quarantine the building.

To complete the illusion, a brightly illuminated HAZMAT van pulls up to the entrance within minutes with its strobe light flashing. The Yellow Radioactive Danger Triangle is displayed prominently on each side. Eight figures clad in what appear to be radiation suits leave through the back door, and they scurry into the laboratory. The two Military Police are positioned in front to ensure that isolation is maintained.

Once the eight are brought inside, the doors are locked, and the Colonel makes his appearance on the balcony of his office loft with his sidekick/concubine standing next to him. They are wearing their dress uniforms to emphasize power—an obvious reflection of his delusionary ego. Sergeant Kelly, adorned in her full Ranger attire with a fixed beret, sashays down the steps. It is her desire to give the disliked NSA agents a more personal greeting.

She quips, "You don't look so smug tonight, agents."

With that, Diane leaps forward, ramming the heel of her left palm up under the Sergeant's chin. Her cuffed right hand pressed into the side of her head. She bends the ranger back over a table, and her beret teeters to the side of her red mane. One of the other guards grabs Diane by the neck and roughly yanks her back to her place in line. Sgt. Kelly rises, fixes her headwear, and sends a vicious slap across the restrained prisoner's mouth, splitting her lip.

"I am going to deal with you myself, bitch," growls the Ranger.

The Colonel doesn't want to risk any distractions and needs this operation to flow smoothly.

"That's enough. Take those four to the conference room and secure them."

Roger looks befuddled. This is so out of character for Diane. She is the most disciplined person he knows. She has never lost control like that before. He wonders if the pressure has finally gotten to her.

As ordered, the prisoners are marched into the conference room and seated in chairs adjacent to one another. Their hands remain cuffed, and one limb is zip-tied twice to a chair leg. When left to themselves, Diane turns to her partner and removes a bobby pin from her mouth. Roger now understands the attack was a charade all designed to extract one of the pins holding the Ranger's beret in place.

Agent Edwards shakes his head, "Diane, you never cease to impress me."

"This should handle the cuffs with ease, but we need something to cut the zip ties."

Ursula speaks, "Will a knife work?"

The agents look at each other with raised eyebrows.

"Well, yes."

"I have one in my pants. I hid it when we tried to escape from the safe house and sort of forgot it was there."

"Good girl, Ursula, things might just be looking up."

"Okay. This is the plan. I spoke to Dr. Allen, and he will try to create some kind of distraction for us at or near level ten. Stay alert. The Colonel more than likely has eyes on us, so I am uncuffing myself and Roger. We must all sit as though we are bound. At the appropriate time, Roger will uncuff you all, and I'll take the knife from Ursula and cut our leg ties. Until then, we wait."

In the main lab, pressure is being placed on Dr. Allen to begin the process. They need five grams of the material within the next twelve hours to meet their obligations. Once control of the lab is ceded back, there's no guarantee they will be able to regain it. This evening is critical for all concerned. Sergeant Kelly tugs on Pamela's dyed hair to provide some incentive.

Cameron, not wanting to lose all bargaining power, yells at the arrogant soldier, "If you hurt her, you can go to hell. I'll never help you."

The Colonel silently motions for the Ranger to ease up on her grip. "Okay, Dr. Allen, this is your show. If you perform, we will all go home happy. If not, well, we shouldn't be discussing that right now, should we?"

"Give me thirty minutes to get familiar with the equipment. I can tell you more once I finish that." Once he has spoken, Cameron begins an intense study of the complex mechanisms and their method of altering the magnetism and temperature of the chamber. He also tries to decipher Brad's method for inserting the Harmonic distortions that were so unique to his studies. Creating two-dimensional space was not easy. The magnetic field must be increased to 100,000, which is the strength of the Earth. Standard methods required absolute zero temperatures, but Mark found a way to do it at higher levels. All he knew about the harmonic resonance process was what he read in the original flash drive. His friend was a genius and a trailblazer in the use of sound. There was no other source of information to learn from. Cam had to manage to deal with all of this in real-time.

Dr. Allen theorized that the fractional quantum Hall effect created a sudden vacuum by changing three-dimensional space into two. It was like a normal vacuum but different in that it removes space itself. We all know nature abhors a vacuum, and when nothing conventional was available to fill it, the exotic material was assumed to be the path of least resistance. Where it originated was anyone's guess, but the leading theory was another dimension. A region is never seen by the human eye or instrument.

Cam also believed that if the substance had been allowed to remain in the void, a natural healing process would have occurred. It was its rapid removal for study or other nefarious purposes that caused this bizarre rift in space to become stable and possibly grow in intensity.

He nervously notifies the Colonel that he is comfortable enough to begin, and Dr. Salazar settles into place alongside him, assisting in any manner possible. The equipment slowly powers up. The desired magnetic field could not be achieved instantly. With current technology, it required multiple incremental increases until the desired level was attained. The magnetic level in phase one reaches 25,000 times that of the earth or one-quarter of the necessary level. He initiates phase two, and the temperature drops down to -100 degrees F.

Level three begins to introduce sound, which attempts to make the space more unstable to facilitate the desired result. Each phase takes ten to fifteen minutes to initiate and an equal amount of time to evaluate before moving on. Levels four and five boost the magnetization up to 50,000 times that of the earth. Half of what is needed. Level six again reduces the temperature to -150 degrees F. Level seven increases the pulse of harmonic distortion.

The computer, as in the past, requests a password, which Cam provides instantly. The laboratory is buzzing with sound and electricity. The "audience" watches this man conduct a symphony of powerful forces, uniting them together with spellbinding coordination. Eventually they will all be focused on an incredibly small area.

The anticipation in the room hangs like a thick blanket over the astonished onlookers. Level eight is reached, and magnetism reaches 75,000 times that of the

Earth. Level nine reduces the temperature just a bit more to -175 degrees F. Cameron is ready to execute the tenth and last level. He looks up to see the salivating Colonel smiling, consumed by greed. Now is the time.

"Colonel, I need more power to get to the final level. Can you provide us with more?"

Dr. Salazar responds first, "We can reroute the building's generator into the equipment. Will that be enough?"

Cam answers. "I think so. We are just shy about what we need."

"I can do it in ten minutes."

Fielding tersely responds, "What are you waiting for? Do it." Visions of his exotic beach life float about his cerebral cortex.

Dr. Salazar returns in less than eight and gives the thumbs-up sign.

There is a small, undetectable smile curling across Dr. Allen's face as he engages in the last phase. Several powerful beams are shot into the containment room. A flash of blinding white light disorients everyone in attendance. Almost simultaneously, he uses his recently obtained control to disable the building's power, throwing it into blackness and virtual chaos. It is the one thing he can do to help the agents and improve their chances of surviving the night.

When the building's lights go out, Diane acts, seeing it as her cue. Using Ursula's knife, she cuts herself free and then moves to Roger. Her partner quickly uses the bobby pin to pick the locks on the other two cuffs while Diane works on freeing their legs. The darkness will give them the element of surprise.

Agent Vitullo, knowing quite well that Roger wants revenge on the two security guards, one of whom tasered him the night before, allows him to roam free. She instructs Brad to locate and detain Dr. Salazar while she goes about settling the score with Sergeant Kelly. She asks Ursula to comfort Pam and take her and Cam out of harm's way. She believes Colonel Fielding will show his true colors and remain out of the fray.

The quartet bursts out of the conference room, and almost immediately, Agent Edwards is face to face with the formerly bespectacled operative who's virtually blind in the darkness. He tries to stop his progress before Roger can grab him, but it's too late. Roger is too angry to deny it. He grabs the man by his lapels and lifts him off the floor before throwing him several feet into a wall. His stunned body slides down to the floor, and the NSA agent is waiting with a well-placed blow to the back of his head. Roger uses his cuffs to bind the man's hands behind his back.

The team spreads out, and Roger goes left toward the main room while Diane and Brad go right, thinking their quarries would try to return to the office. The assumptions each makes are correct, and after a minor scuffle, Dr. Salazar is latched to a pipe. Diane rushes past an outcove, and Sgt. Kelly emerges behind her, slamming a hard blow to the back of her neck.

The agent drops to her knees, stunned, and the sergeant tugs her head back by the hair and sends a punch down her jaw. As she readies a second blow, Diane grabs her leg, yanking it outward and toppling the Ranger to her back. A kick is aimed, but Vitullo manages to dodge it and rise to her feet, holding her foe's ankle. She tugs her close and delivers a kick of her own. The dazed soldier is unable to avoid the second kick that sends her into dreamland. She is also cuffed in place.

Brad and Diane then seek to locate the Colonel, trying to find their way up to his office in the blackness.

Agent Edwards finally locates the guard who tazed him last night. An angry Edwards is not to be messed with. The man displays a total lack of wisdom and assumes a martial arts stance. This offers no deterrence, and the agent plods forward, blocking one blow and shrugging off the next as he swings his powerful right arm outward. You can hear the cracking of the poor man's jaw as his body drops quickly to the concrete floor. Not one to normally lose his cool, Roger sends a hard kick into the fallen foe's ribs, then slams his head into the floor, ending his night.

When the combat ceases, and the dust settles, the chopping blades of a helicopter can be heard on the roof. Vitullo and Jones are closest, making their way outside just in time to see a UH-60 Blackhawk rise off the parapet and veer out into the night sky. The uniformed frame of Colonel Fielding was clearly inside.

Knowing they are too late to prevent his escape, Diane realizes they must attend to Dr. Allen and the two women. They also must call headquarters to seal the lab and clean up the disabled bodies inside. Hopefully, some intelligence can be gathered through interrogation.

The six are reunited outside the containment room. Cameron and Pamela are entwined in a tight embrace. Tears are flowing freely. Ursula stands back, so happy for the blissful ending. Diane turns and notices that there is some energy between the sister-in-law and her partner. She tries to disguise the smirk on her face before it is noticed.

The anomaly is still present but appears to be fuzzy or somewhat blurred in appearance.

"I was able to place a magnetic shell or casing around it. This should keep it stable until we figure out how to deal with it on a more permanent basis."

"Is everyone ok?" asks Agent Vitullo.

The assembled all nod in the affirmative.

"I can't thank you enough, doctor, for all you have done. You're a true hero and a true patriot."

A sack is found with all the hostage's belongings. Weapons, wallets, and cell phones. Diane quickly rushes to her phone to see two messages from Dr. Parisi. She ducks away to return the call. Minutes later, she returns to wrap up the scene.

"Thank you, agents, for keeping Pamela safe. I apologize for my stupidity earlier. I only made the situation worse by not listening to you."

"You did what you thought was right, Doctor. I can't fault you for that."

"Roger, can you get a hold of Myles? We need to brief him and get a team down here to clean this place up." The detectives get Myles on a conference call and relay the bizarre events of the last several days.

"Okay, agents, listen up; we need to get rooms for our guests to sleep tonight. I have commandeered the ParTec Gulfstream to take everyone back to DC tomorrow."

Roger offers his place for the night, and Ursula quickly accepts. Diane raises an eyebrow and agrees to let Cameron and Pamela spend the night in her guestroom.

"Brad, the sofa is open if you want it."

Myles ends with, "I want everyone to go home, get a good night's sleep, and be here at 9:00 AM for a complete debriefing, after which you can all head back to the Capital. Kristen Dryden and Colonel Fielding are still on the loose. I want both in cells by week's end. Am I clear, agents?"

"Yes, sir, we can't wait to see Ms. Dryden again."

Cars are sent to the lab to chauffeur the parties to their designated abodes.

Diane and her guests arrive at the Mode and realize they are famished. She suggests they order takeout from the 90 Miles Cuban Café on Armitage, only several hundred feet from the apartment. She places the order by phone and pays with a credit card. Brad volunteers to make the walk to pick it up.

When Brad leaves, she places another call to "Doctor Dreamy." They chat for fifteen minutes while he is gone. Her body tingles from just the sound of his voice. She notifies him that she will be back in DC tomorrow, and plans are made for a romantic dinner. The explanation will be made in person.

Brad returns, and they devour the food quickly. Their conversation is muted by fatigue, and the lovebirds are eager to retire to the guestroom. They are yearning to get 'reacquainted.' Diane sets out a blanket and pillow for Brad, then goes into her own bedroom. Her mind is still unsettled. She knows they still haven't figured this thing out yet. There is another player in this game. They just don't know who he or she is.

She broods over the scheme and how ParTec was able to acquire the merchandise at little to no cost. Who has the power to accomplish that? Where would the money come from? What's missing from this puzzle?

Diane looks at the photograph of her teenage self with her parents sitting on the dresser. She silently beseeches their assistance. Since their death, she has maintained an old shoebox filled with pages of old FBI paraphernalia. She sorts through the box when something catches her eye. She dismisses the thought, but it, along with some other clues, has aroused her suspicion. Diane silently rejected Roger's theory that the perpetrator was in the Pentagon.

She believes he resides at another institution. A second dinner with her uncle would need to be planned if she hoped to learn more. The last proved quite beneficial. She silently hopes this one will be of equal value. His assistance might be the only thing that could solve this case.

Chapter 45
Tuesday 11:00 PM, Chanute Airbase (abandoned)

The Blackhawk helicopter speeds through the night, carrying Colonel Fielding to the pre-arranged extraction point. He is lost in thought. His visions of scantily clad Asian teens on the beach are now a thing of the past. Escaping the law and those pit-bull NSA agents are all that is on his mind.

How could he be so stupid? Duped by a pencil-pushing geek genius. He was snookered into giving him control of the building's power. How obvious. It was the one thing that could level the playing field and allow the agents to escape unnoticed. Needing more power was such a clever ruse, and he fell for it hook, line, and sinker. The distraction disoriented his team. It was the only edge the NSA agents needed. His personnel were quickly routed and left lying bound in unconscious heaps.

For a moment, he pictures the sexy little Sergeant in handcuffs, and the demented part of him is aroused. But he has no time for idle thoughts right now. He needs an excuse—someone to point the blame at. Ice will not be happy to hear about the night's events, but he has served him well for many years. He was a vital cog in his pursuit of wealth. That would surely be rewarded. But he needed to be convincing and self-assured if he hoped to get the assistance he needed. The mastermind would solve his legal issues and provide him with a safe flight from justice. He would still be able to enjoy an exciting life with the earnings he stashed over the last decade. Just not as spectacular as the one he envisioned only hours ago.

The helicopter sets down on the vacant weed-infested tarmac that was once a bustling airfield. The military had long since abandoned this base in a series of closures at the end of the Cold War. All that remains is a shell of empty deteriorating buildings and a rumpled airstrip. He expects to see a car or plane sitting by to take him on the next leg of his journey.

The pilot yells out, "Colonel, we have landed. I need to get this bird back to Scott Airforce Base in St. Claire. I don't have any fuel to spare, sir. I'll need you to exit."

The door is opened for him, and he steps out onto the unkempt runway. Both the Colonel and the Airbase are now mere ghosts of their former selves. He scans the area intently, searching for his next link.

The moonless night is dark, and when his phone buzzes, it casts the only light for yards. He gazes down at the screen.

COLONEL FIELDING, DO YOU HAVE MY MERCHANDISE?

NO, SIR, DR. ALLEN DECEIVED US. HE TRICKED DR. SALAZAR INTO GIVING HIM CONTROL OF THE BUILDING POWER. I WOULD NEVER HAVE AGREED TO THAT SIR.

HOW DID THAT EFFECT US, COLONEL?

HE CUT POWER AND BLINDED US. THE AGENTS USED DARKNESS TO OVERPOWER OUR SECURITY. WE LOST CONTROL OF THE FACILITY.

SO, YOU FAILED ME?

WE WERE NOT SUCCESSFUL, BUT I HAVE THE PLAN TO GET THE MATERIAL ALREADY PRODUCED. JUST GIVE ME SOME TIME. WHERE IS MY RIDE, SIR? IS A CAR ON THE WAY?

COLONEL FIELDING, YOUR NEXT JOURNEY WILL NOT REQUIRE A CAR.

With the utterance of those words, a bullet is fired by a sniper with a high-powered rifle. In less than a second, it pierces Fielding's skull at the temple, killing him instantly. His 6'3" frame collapses on the ground and lies motionless in a pool of blood. Perhaps a fitting end for one so despicable. It is poetic justice that a shell of a once-promising military officer meets his fate in the shell of a once-prominent military facility.

Chapter 46

Wednesday 9:00 AM, NSA Headquarters, Undisclosed location, Chicago, IL

As demanded, Diane and Roger arrived at Headquarters accompanied by their fellow hostages. To avoid the wrath of their boss, they each pull up thirty minutes early.

Myles had requested written reports from all six former prisoners, with the agents subject to an oral debriefing immediately following. They both enter the small office used for said purpose and take seats. The director preferred individual interrogations, but it was in the middle of the fiscal budget process, and time was short. For that reason, a joint meeting was conducted.

"Now tell me, agents, how did this go down."

Diane begins recounting Kristen's late-night call and her plea for rescue. She admits that they were duped, knowing Myles would find out anyway. The capture of Brad and Pamela made simple in their absence is also divulged. They then detail the transport to the plane and meet up with Dr. Allen and Ursula on the runway at Reagan National. Diane took great pains to praise Cam for his intelligence and courage. He also had pretty good instincts for a civilian. The ingenuity used to nullify the anomaly and cut the power was downright amazing.

The conversation then shifted to ParTec Industries and everything the agents had dug up during the nearly two-week investigation.

"We know what happened, director, but we don't know who or how it was carried out. I am also curious about a comment from the Asian mercenary. She told me she would have killed me but was ordered not to. I am unable to explain that."

"Forget it, Diane," responds Myles, "they probably didn't want the heat associated with offing a fed."

"I get the feeling it was more involved, sir, but perhaps we will learn more when we find the ringleader."

"Do we have any suspects?"

Roger responds by signaling his belief that it is Pentagon-related. He is working on his contacts to learn more. Diane disagrees but keeps mum, not wanting to contradict her partner.

"I am checking on some other leads. Let's see if anything pans out."

"Okay, agents, get back to DC and do your best to end this mess. I am still getting heat from the local office. The quicker Dryden and Fielding are apprehended, the better this will be for all of us. You have great instincts, Vitullo, but don't get reckless. This was a complex organization. Ruthless and intelligent, be careful."

The director resumes speaking after taking a swig from a warm bottle of spring water.

"Since you were in custody, I am not sure you heard. Uncle Trevor will be installed as director on Friday. Now go do your job. I will be busy with budget meetings for the rest of the day. Your plane will be ready at noon."

"Thank you, sir."

"And by the way, good job, agents."

Diane had packed for her date that evening but brought an extra suit just in case the next call is successful. She dials his private number.

"Uncle Trevor, I am calling to congratulate you on becoming the country's top spook. I hear you get installed on Friday. I'd love to reciprocate on dinner to celebrate and thank you for Fermi."

"Diane, my love, it is always great hearing from you, but seeing you is exponentially better. How does tomorrow evening, at the same time and in the same place, sound?"

"See you then, Uncle Trevor. I feel the same."

Roger listens to his partner making dinner plans and walks over to Diane's desk. Her jacket and holster are hung over the back of the chair. He removes his cell phone from his pocket and presses a few keys until he hears the correct tone. When he finished, he discreetly returned to his cubicle.

With the debriefings complete and the director's schedule filled with budget issues, there is nothing more to do. The group assembles in the lobby and waits for their ride to DuPage Airport and the ensuing flight to DC.

Pamela agrees to stay with Cameron at his place in the Channel Apartments. Ursula invites Roger to bunk at her home in Chevy Case. Brad, ever the gentleman, offers Diane a room in his residence on Fourth Place. She thanks the Detective but blushingly hopes that his offer isn't necessary.

With sleeping arrangements settled, they boarded the shuttle. The six have been through quite an ordeal these past few days. They have weathered a fierce storm and grown close, bonding together in the face of danger.

When the shuttle returns to the airport, they exit the vehicle and reenter the Gulfstream—this time not as handcuffed prisoners but as conquering heroes.

In mid-flight, a pensive Dr. Allen turns to the two agents and begins to speak.

"Can I trust you, agents?"

Roger responds, "Dr. Allen, you definitely earned it."

"I never discussed the original flash drive. I have it hidden where no one will find it, but I am not certain it is something the world is ready for. If this material is used in war, it will destroy our planet."

Diane interjects, "Think of what eight ounces could do in the hands of a terrorist. It is totally untraceable."

"Do you both agree we should destroy it."

The agents look at each other. If used properly, the energy potential of this particle could revolutionize industry and life on the planet. But one fatal error would bring about a global catastrophe. They each look for a reason to refute his premise, but neither can. Both agents have personally benefitted from the wisdom this man has displayed in the recent past. They look at each other and nod in the affirmative.

Pamela voices an enthusiastic approval from an aisle away. This vile force has taken one man from her. She doesn't want to risk another.

"Okay, it's agreed. When we get back, one of you will accompany me to where it is hidden, and we will destroy it once and for all. Perhaps a day will come when mankind is responsible enough to wield this power."

Roger takes the lead, "I know your plate is full in DC, Diane. Let me go with the doctor. You really don't need to cross the line again with Myles by destroying evidence. I will bring Brad with me, and the three of us can rid the world of this plague."

"That, partner, sounds like a plan."

Chapter 47

Wednesday 4:00 PM, The National Mall, Washington, DC

It's a clear, sunny afternoon in the nation's capital as Diane separates from the group. She needs some time alone to reflect on the recent events at Fermi. She always found it better to pull back when things started moving too fast. They were successful this time. Was it skill or luck? Roger, Cam, and Brad will deal with the flash drive. They were good and capable people. Without them, she would not have been able to close Fermi's case. The world is safe for now, but for how long? Filled with gloom she strides past 14th Street, glancing up and the Washington Monument standing erect as it reaches up to the blue sky. Her thoughts were heavy in contrast to the weather. This is the city where her parents were ruthlessly slaughtered in a violent street crime in an upscale neighborhood. She feels their presence like they are here trying to warn her of something. She just can't decipher what it means. Their influence is closer than it ever has been since that fateful evening. Are they alerting her to an evil, ominous force present in this city? If so, who is pulling the strings? Deep down inside, Diane feels she should have already solved this case. Her subconscious mind is keeping something from her. Why is she fighting her instincts now after all these years?

Doubts fill her every thought. Questions abound. Can we make any place safe? Is she or the agency doing any real good in the world? When will the next Pandora particle appear, and what will it look like? The universe seems dark to her now. Evil at every turn, just waiting to pounce on the innocent. Shadows block out the sunshine. She feels a bit overwhelmed, as if Justice is running on a treadmill. The speed is continuously increasing. The pace is constantly intensifying. She pushes herself sweating and panting but getting nowhere. Even though she is walking comfortably, her breathing is labored—her heart races.

The tree-lined path brings her to the Martin Luther King Memorial, and those who died for a cause are recalled. Just when it seems that the sinister side has won, and her frayed spirit is at the breaking point, she arrives at the mammoth marble statue of Abraham Lincoln A class of grade school children march in a tight line in front of her, clad in their plaid school uniforms. The teacher keeps a tight rein on the group, careful not to let any wander astray. The sound of their laughter fills the sidewalk. Their gleeful faces were enjoying every last second of the day. They deserve a bright future and the right to be happy. This is why she does what she does. With renewed focus, she begins to regain her resolve and reevaluates the case at hand. Determined to make right this wrong. Something was off. Who had the authority to requisite all that hardware and make it disappear? She was dealing with a level of power shared only among the few. The culprit must come from a select elite. ParTec Industries was gone, but unless they got to the root of the problem, it would manifest itself in another form. Millions would be stolen from the treasury, possibly funding countless dangerous experiments. Tomorrow night, she had a chance to enter that upper stratum. She needed a glimpse of how that world worked. Her last dinner got her into Fermi, and she hopes tomorrow night will follow suit. Perhaps her "Uncle" could open another door.

Diane glances down at her watch, noticing it is past 5:00 PM. She smiles thinking of the other reason for optimism. The tall, handsome Doctor will be her companion this evening. Her lips curl into a smile as "date" enters her mind. She doesn't remember the last one but feels it went wrong. That will not happen this evening. She knows they have a connection. One last glance is taken at the massive edifice before she scurries back to Detective Jones's house. She wants to look perfect tonight.

Chapter 48

Wednesday 7:00 PM, Restaurant Tosca, 1112 F Street, Washington, DC

Diane arrived at the restaurant at 7:05 PM, taking a cab from Brad's house, where she showered and primped for the big evening. She always had 'Hollywood' looks, but when dressed to impress, she could absolutely dazzle. Her 'just the right length' cocktail dress straddled the line between classy and flirtatious with perfect grace. Dr. William Parisi was already seated when she made her entrance, and what an entrance it was. Every head in the restaurant turned as she nervously strolled to the handsome Doctor's table.

He rises to greet her, and they embrace in a lingering hug punctuated with him whispering, "I missed you so."

She responds with an almost inaudible, "I thought about you a lot."

"Good thoughts, I hope?"

That question was answered with a smile.

The two well-seasoned adults behaved like nervous prom dates. It was hard to tell who blushed more. Diane stayed with her usual red wine and allowed Will to make the selection. He opted for an expensive French burgundy, which they sipped between compliments. Time seemed frozen with the universe on pause until an impatient waiter interrupted the mutual revelry.

Diane appeased him by ordering the fresh catch while the Doctor countered with the seafood pasta. How they were able to eat without taking their eyes off each other was a minor miracle. They finished with a scrumptious tiramisu dessert, which was shared. Limoncello topped off the meal, and both sat lost in each other's eyes until the same waiter deposited the check on the table between them, disturbing the silence.

Diane offers to pay the bill in appreciation of the assistance he provided in the mercenary's capture.

His reply, "You're walking into my life more than equals anything I did," sends chills down her spine.

"Where are you staying tonight?" asks Will.

"Brad offered his place, but I haven't committed."

"Are you looking for a better offer?"

She looks up to see an impish grin on his face.

"Perhaps."

"Consider one submitted."

Will Parisi stands up as he's speaking those words and offers his arm to escort her from the table. Diane accepts with a wide smile, and they walk out together toward the valet.

Chapter 49

Thursday 9:00 AM, Gallery 64 Apartments, 64 H Street, Washington, DC

Diane awakens in the main bedroom of an apartment in the Gallery 64 building on H Street. She cannot remember the last time she arose in the bed of a man. She also can't remember the last time she felt so good. When her body rolls to the left, she realizes that her partner has already arisen. The aroma of bacon sizzling on the stove offers a clue as to his location.

She slides her long legs off the bed and dons the robe left out for her, gracious for the clothing but suspicious of how many others have worn it. Wiping the haze from her eyes, she follows her nose into the kitchen. As if accused by a mere look, Dr. Will stammered a defense.

"I bought that robe, a pair of jeans, and a sweatshirt yesterday."

She is somewhat amused to see his coolness melt as he begins to squirm a bit under pressure.

Diane decides to have a little fun with the moment.

"So, you thought of me as a sure thing?"

His face reddens, and she cannot continue the ruse, bursting into laughter. When he realizes what's happening, he joins her.

"Well, then, I guess the cooking lessons are over the top."

She appreciates the quick recovery and the modest-sized kitchen echoes with laughter.

Agent Vitullo cannot remember when she has laughed so much or felt so comfortable in the presence of another man save for her partner. Oh, shoot, she murmurs to herself, I need to call Roger. They are meeting Brad for lunch today.

Will and Diane sit down for breakfast. The mood they set last night carries on undiminished. Will tells Diane he must be at work by noon and is pulling a double. His shift won't end until after midnight.

He sees the frown forming on her face and pulls a key from his pocket. She smiles and takes possession without hesitation. The doctor is made aware of the agent's schedule, and the dinner with her uncle set for this evening. She admits she wouldn't mind coming by after the meal in McLean to resume what they have begun.

"You have the key. Come back anytime."

They hug and return to the bedroom to dress. A kiss leads to more, and they are slightly detoured in their quest to clothe. His arms envelop her, and she shudders, surrendering to his embrace. He lifts her off the floor, and their bodies collapse onto the bed. Thirty minutes later, Diane emerges in a state of near euphoria. She is clad in jeans and a Georgetown sweatshirt, looking a bit out of place with the spiked heels she wore last night. Roger is telephoned just a bit late, and they agree to meet at a restaurant called Easy Company on the wharf at noon.

A quick call to Brad follows with a plea for him to bring a comfortable pair of flats from her bag. She then graciously accepts Will's offer to drop her off on his way to the hospital.

Chapter 50

Thursday 12:00 PM, Easy Company Wine Bar, 98 Blair Alley SW, Washington, DC

Roger and Brad look out the window from their table inside the restaurant. They watch keenly as the pricey BMW pulls up to the entrance, and Diane, in jeans and a sweatshirt, ambles up the pathway in her spiked heels. Both men roar with laughter.

When she arrives at the table, Roger greets her with, "That is the most elegant walk of shame I have ever seen."

The three laugh together.

"Funny, Roger, I'll be sure to tell Ursula you're a sexist pig. How is the Chevy Chase soiree going?"

"Touche, Diane."

Brad snickers and Roger quickly snarls, "Don't even think about going there, cupcake."

"Okay enough, let's get to work."

Roger opens, "My Pentagon sources are coming up empty. I am getting nowhere fast. Seems like whoever is orchestrating this is a ghost."

Those words seem to register with Diane, and for a fleeting moment, she is lost in thought.

"We came up empty locally as well. We still have an APB out on the sister, Kristen Dryden, but as of now, it's crickets."

"Well, I am hoping I can get something out of my uncle at dinner tonight. He should be in a good mood, given his promotion, and I'll shower him with appreciation for the access to Fermi. What's up with the real flash drive? That is of vital importance."

"As soon as we are finished here, Brad and I are picking up Doctor Allen at the Institute and heading to the hiding place, where it will be destroyed immediately by one of us, with the other two serving as witnesses."

"I'll be happy when that is done. Be careful you are not followed, and text me to confirm."

"Will do." The mutual response is uttered together.

"Myles isn't going to let us stay here forever, so we need to make some progress soon. Why don't you two pay the accountant a visit? Roger might be able to pressure him into a mistake with those gorilla hands. I need to get to the library to do some more research on Gunther and get some FBI records. Be careful, guys. We are going to be stepping on some powerful toes soon."

Diane, having just finished breakfast, sips on an iced tea while her companions devour their hamburgers with carnivorous fervor.

"We have come this far; I have no intention of failing now."

They all agree and plan to meet tomorrow morning at 10:00 AM at a place to be determined.

Before leaving, Diane asks Brad if she could dress at his house for her dinner tonight. He happily agrees to her proposition and offers his car as transportation. She declines.

"An Uber will do me good."

"She needs some humbling after being chauffeured in that BMW. It's way out of her league," teases Roger.

"Funny, guys, real funny."

When lunch is finished, Diane leaves to do some research, and Roger and Brad pick up Dr. Allen for their delayed but very important task.

Chapter 51

Thursday 7:00 PM, J Gilberts Wood Fired Steaks and Seafood, 6930 Old Dominion Drive, McLean, VA

Diane exits the Uber in a pinstriped charcoal suit with matching tights. Alluring yet professional. Underneath her jacket was a light grey mock and the ever-present holster encasing her Glock. She arrives to see Uncle Trevor already waiting for her at his private booth. He's never early, so this is a bit surprising. She sees him wave and makes her way to the table.

After a big hug, he says, "Please sit down, my dear. I'm so glad you invited me to dinner. It's always good to see family."

After they embrace, Diane takes a seat next to him.

"I hope you don't mind. I took the liberty of ordering you a dirty martini."

"Wonderful."

"Now, I was hoping you could fill me in on the Fermi case. Was my interview able to provide any assistance with the investigation? Have you made any arrests?"

"Yes, on both accounts, Uncle Trevor. Your interview provided us with access to the inner workings of the lab. We subsequently arrested several individuals, two of whom we think were responsible for the deaths of Dr. Stanton and Dr. Millstead. We also found out that some exotic material was created and was scheduled to be sold on the black market for a king's ransom. In addition, the dangerous anomaly which lingered from Dr. Stanton's work was neutralized. I'd have to say it was a good day's work. The only negative was that Colonel Fielding escaped by helicopter."

"Well, that must be quite a feather in your cap. I certainly hope you are proud of your accomplishment."

"I would say so, but we uncovered something we still can't put together. A company called ParTec Industries was able to source government property and weapons at little to no cost. We know the Colonel was highly involved in the supply chain. We believe he provided the company with a list of what was to be bid on. They somehow sourced the material without paying and were able to underbid the competition. We believe they made approximately one hundred eighty million dollars over a ten-year period."

"What you're saying is fascinating, Diane. Fascinating but alarming. Do you have any leads?"

"My partner believes it is a source inside the Pentagon, and he is working his contacts."

"And what do you think dear? I am sensing that you disagree."

"Your senses are correct, Uncle. I think the accomplice is located somewhere within the CIA. It had to be purchased with black ops budgets to stay off the books. I have hesitated to begin any investigation because I do not want to raise any alarms that would jeopardize your appointment. It's the reason I am here tonight. I could use your help."

"You really believe it starts in the CIA?"

"I'm sorry, sir, but I really do. I believe it's someone with close ties to Gunther Dryden, the founder of ParTec Industries."

"I will make this the top priority on my agenda as Director. We can't allow this to occur on my watch."

The martinis arrive and are placed in front of them. Trevor thanks the waiter and Diane reaches for her glasses.

"Sorry, sweetheart, but I think he reversed our drinks. I am trying the blue cheese olives tonight."

They exchange cocktails, and each takes a sip.

"I noticed Gunther went to the University of Pittsburgh while you were there. Did you know him or ever meet him?"

"I can't say I recall the name, Diane."

She continues while taking another sip of the ice-cold liquid. "He also played football for two years." Diane tries to see if there are any reactions on Trevor's face, but his expression reveals nothing. She sits in disbelief that she is posing these questions to the man who looked after her in a time of need.

"Interesting, you are quite thorough, Agent Vitullo."

Suddenly, Diane felt flush. She begins to perspire, and her vision blurs. "I'm sorry, uncle, suddenly I don't feel that good."

"What's wrong, dear?"

She feels dizzy, and the room spins around her head. Her hands begin to shake, and she tries blinking madly to restore her vision, tightly gripping her napkin. She fights nausea until she finally slumps back in her chair, eyes glazed.

"Waiter, my niece has taken ill; we need to leave."

Trevor places a one-hundred-dollar bill on the table and lifts his adopted daughter from her seat to usher her toward the door while dialing his phone. Diane's feet practically drag across the carpet as she is transported to the exit.

"Bring the car around now."

He carries the dazed detective outside and opens the rear passenger door, placing her in the back seat. Then, he walks around the vehicle and enters the opposite side.

"You know where to go," he barks at the driver.

A female voice replies, "Yes, sir, right away."

Chapter 52

Thursday 9:00 PM, NSA Headquarters
Undisclosed location, Chicago, IL

Myles Warner returns to the office after a short dinner break. He pours himself a cup of stale coffee and sits at his desk. The pile of files lying in wait is almost overwhelming. His budget obligations have kept him from his normal duties for far too long. It was time to sort through the mess. He looks at his wristwatch. It was going to be a long night, and he might as well start sooner rather than later.

After resolving some more complicated matters requiring some intricate and tedious thought, he notices the stack of written debriefing reports from the Fermi case. He sees this as an opportunity to maximize his now-limited attention span. Reviewing these should be a formality and clear up much of his desk.

A report from the FBI crime lab was on the top of the pile. He remembers Diane's insistence on him getting Admiral Wilson's insulin bottles dusted for prints. He lifts the folder, opens it, and reads.

FBI Crime Lab report:

Fingerprints taken from eight bottles of insulin recovered in the residence of the deceased Admiral Wilson, Director of the Central Intelligence Agency.

Findings: Four of the bottles were found to have the fingerprints of two individuals hereby identified as:

CIA Director, Admiral Clarence Wilson.

Deputy CIA Director, Trevor Hawthorne.

The remaining four bottles had the sole prints of Admiral Clarence Wilson.

This struck Myles as odd. He questioned what Diane was looking for, but it raised no immediate alarm.

He opens the next folder, which is Dr. Cameron Allen's debriefing file. His face literally freezes when he reads of Cameron's phone call with Trevor Hawthorne, leading to his ultimate capture and imprisonment. The two cannot be coincidences. His heartbeat rises to unprecedented levels, and he feels a chilling sweat drench his body. He immediately dials Diane's cell phone to warn her of the threat that her dinner date poses. A voicemail is left. He leaves a text message for his agent but doesn't wait for a reply. Myles immediately dials Agent Edwards but, after numerous rings, gets no response.

He detests the next move he is forced to make, but Diane's safety is paramount. "Hello, Director Crawford. This is Myles Warner, Director Chicago."

"I know who you are, Myles, but why are you calling me at this hour?"

"My agent is in danger. Deputy Director Hawthorne is the mole. I have proof."

"That would be the agent operating in my territory without my knowledge. I don't give a rat's ass about her director."

"It's no time to be petty, Sheila. Her life may be in danger. Hawthorne is dangerous."

"If you think I'm going after the soon-to-be Director of the CIA with this crap, you're even crazier than I thought. Good night, Myles."

The director is in a near panic mode when he remembers the young police detective. Files are tossed left and right until the one labeled Lt. Brad Allen comes into view. He finds a cell phone number and presses seven digits. Brad awakens from a sound sleep to the buzzing of his phone. Informed of the situation, he dresses hastily and searches for his car keys. He must get to the restaurant as soon as possible. On his way to the car, he unsuccessfully attempts to reach Roger.

He starts the engine and heads to I-395 to connect with the George Washington Parkway. At this hour, he thinks he can get there in fifteen minutes. His mind races, and he then, in a eureka moment, dials Ursula's phone, hoping she can get to Roger.

She answers, "Ursula, is Roger there? Diane is in big trouble."

"I'll get him."

Roger's voice rumbles on the phone, "It's late, cupcake. Did you miss me?"

"Diane is in danger; Trevor is the ringleader."

"Oh shit, where's my phone? I have a tracer on her. Damn, my phone is dead. I'll meet you at the restaurant and charge it on the way."

He turns to Ursula, asking to borrow her car. She threw him the keys, and he raced at breakneck speed down I-495.

Eighteen minutes later, the two converge in the empty parking lot of the closed J. Gilberts Restaurant. Roger jumps into Brad's car and reengages the USB port. They wait for his phone to reach a sufficient power level. Each second that passes feels like an eternity.

Chapter 53

Thursday 10:00 PM, Safe House, Scotts Run Rd., McLean, VA

Diane is carried into the safe house and left sprawled on the sofa. Her heels are removed and left on the floor. They take off her jacket and holster and place them at the end of the room on a small kitchen table. Trevor and his female companion sit and wait for their captive to stir. Their captive lies motionless for several minutes, succumbing to the sophisticated drug's effects. They wane slowly, and soon Diane awakens. She is disoriented and drowsy but conscious. Opening her eyes, she scans the room, trying to focus on her captors. She recalls the dinner with her uncle and somehow expects to see him there. He is seated with folded legs in an armchair across the room. The silhouette of his figure is immediately recognizable. She squints, trying to identify his female accomplice. It takes several more moments for her vision to be clear enough to discern the driver's attributes. She recognizes the hair and the face and searches in the shallows of her brain for a name. Then recognition arrives. The person standing there is none other than Kristen Dryden.

Her uncle initiates the dialogue, "Hello Diane, I believe introductions are in order."

"I know who she is, Trevor."

"Ah, I am no longer Uncle Trevor. So be it."

"Well, drugging me has sort of put me at odds."

"Well, dear Diane, I believe I need to fill you in just a bit more family history. You are aware that you are my adopted daughter, but what you don't know is that Kristen is my biological offspring."

Diane's jaw drops in utter disbelief her body sways unsteadily, "What are you saying?" She cannot believe what she is hearing.

"You see, her mother, Marsha, and I were lovers way before Gunther entered the picture. Kristen, here was the fruit of that relationship. My old school chum, whom I carried financially, was adept at playing the fool. I even moved them here to Virginia so Marsha would be close to me. It took him some time, but he finally found out about the affair. I don't know how he found out, but he did approximately five years ago. Lacking coping skills, he angrily confronted dear Marsha as if he were someone in her league. The idiot actually thought she could love him. Depending on whose account you believe, she either was pushed or fell down the stairs, breaking her neck. A very short-sighted act on his part, don't you agree, Kristen? She nods her head in the affirmative.

Nevertheless, it was time to remove him from the operation. I gave the order for his termination and Kristen, ever eager to please me, volunteered to carry it out. It was made to look like they both perished in an auto accident so that no inquiries would be made." A clever ruse she concocted, if I must say.

Diane listens, trying to cope with this new distorted version of reality. Her mind numbs. "This can't be real. How can all of this have happened?"

"Oh, but it is Diane. It is indeed true."

Kristen rises from her seat. She is dressed in a mid-length khaki skirt, button-down eggshell top, and brown tights. She slowly begins to step out of her heels.

"Now Diane, I need to know where the original flash drive is. I have obligations to fulfill. You know as well as I that I will get it one way or another. Let me have the drive, and I will let you live. We do not have to do this the hard way. If you resist my dear Kristen is here to provide any needed incentive."

"I'll never tell you, Trevor, you're a filthy piece of shit. How could you betray your country and your oath?"

"Well, Diane, in full disclosure, I guess you should be aware of everything that has transpired in our past before calling me names. After all, I am responsible for the murder of your parents. Kristen has known about you and hated you for years. Something of a sibling rivalry. She really wants you to resist. I urge you not to."

Diane's brain is about to explode, "What? You were their best friend. How could you be?" Visions of the photograph on her nightstand fill her head, distorted by rushing waves of chaos. The very fabric of her reality is unfurling.

Your father was so damn loyal to the Bureau. When he accidentally stumbled onto my extracurricular activities, I gave him an out. My offer to piece him in was quite generous. He would have been an equal partner. But the idiot refused. I never understood his blind loyalty to a cold-hearted bureaucracy. An agency that cared little for anyone. The night of my dinner, he foolishly gave me an ultimatum of twenty-four hours to turn myself in. He thought that I would surrender at the height of my power. How foolish. So,

I telephoned Dryden's house to warn them. My little girl here overhead the conversation and took it upon herself to intercept them on their way home to end the threat. She saved me from a difficult but necessary decision. Dead men tell no tales."

Diane's body stiffens, "She murdered my parents?"

Kristen responds, "Yes, Diane, they were my first kill. I will never forget their screams as I cut their throats. We had to make it look like a violent street crime. It was so arousing."

Diane doesn't know how to react. She is torn between the betrayal of her uncle and the vile fiend who murdered her parents. The suddenness of standing face to face with pure evil is overwhelming. Her body starts to tremble and shake as an uncontrollable rage begins to brew inside of her. A tempest of grief and anger swirls violently within her soul. The sheer intensity of her emotions finally percolates into action, and she rushes forward, sending her left fist into the jaw of the murderess.

Kristen just steps back and smiles. She nods to Trevor after the first punch as if waiting a lifetime for this moment. She blocks Dianes' second attempt and steps forward, rocking the tall detective with a blow to the cheekbone and another to the ribs. Smirking like the rival sibling, she smiles as Diane staggers backward, gleefully pursuing her quarry. The brunette is hit with another punch on the temple, followed by a well-placed kick to the gut. The air rushes from her mouth, and it drives her back to the sofa. Moving catlike, Kristen grabs Vitullo's mock top and lifts her quickly off the cushion, then throws her hard against the wall. Diane's back slams into the unforgiving partition, and she leans against it, stunned, only to be struck by a firm knee in her abdomen, which causes her to double over. An uppercut sends spittle flying and hair billowing. With legs quivering, her tall frame leans back against the wall, trying to cope with her assailant's fury. Kristen's face reveals her lust for violence and her hatred of Diane.

Trevor calls out, "Where is the flash drive, Diane? It will only get worse for you."

Now tasting her own blood, she answers, "Go to hell, Trevor."

"I should not have underestimated you, Diane. I gave you the Fermi lead to keep you in Chicago. I didn't want you here. This all could have been avoided. Why did you have to be such a good detective?"

Kristen looks at him, and he nods. She takes that as a signal to continue. The sick wiring of her brain equates violence with erotic pleasure.

Diane attempts to fight back by extending her left arm and ramming the heel of her palm under Dryden's chin. This forces her head back, but it also leaves the agent's torso exposed. A well-executed kick has Diane gasping for air. She thinks she hears her rib crack, and she feels her long legs beginning to give way. Her back slides down the wall. This allows Kristen to raise her right leg and press her foot into the exposed throat of her prey. It presses her against the wall, and she hangs in limbo. All incoming air is cut off. Diane's face reddens as her lungs empty. The lack of oxygen makes her dizzy.

Kristen then demands to know the location of the flash drive, which is answered by Diane's middle finger. If nothing else, Trevor always knew his daughter relished violence, but only now does he learn how much she adores domination.

She lingers in this pose, thoroughly enjoying the moment. Only when Diane's eyelids begin to flutter does Kristen remove her foot and allow her gasping foe to slide down to a sitting position, legs splayed outward. Her ankle is grabbed, and her limp body is dragged to the center of the room. Resistance is minimal. A wicked smirk adorns Kristen's face as she sends a stomp into the panting heap at her feet. The shockwave ripples through poor Diane. Then, adding insult to injury, she steps on her face in sheer mockery, emphasizing her control and hoping to break the agent's will.

"You're running out of time, Agent Vitullo."

There is no response, so Kristen opts for a handful of hair and a tight grip on Diane's top to raise the statuesque brunette to her feet once again. Diane's legs dangle under her like cooked spaghetti. She hangs, swaying in her tormentor's grasp. Then, she is dragged by the hair to the chair of her seated uncle. Trapped in a full nelson, their eyes meet. Kristen is in total control, manipulating her dazed foe in any manner she chooses.

"You know I have killed everyone who stood in my way, and I will kill you if you don't give me what I want."

"You killed the Admiral too, didn't you?"

"I was tired of being number two, dear."

"I had the FBI dust his insulin, and they will find your prints."

"Do you really think that I can't handle the FBI? Have you not been paying attention?"

When the Deputy Director again requests the location of the flash drive, Diane responds with another expletive and spits in Trevor's face. This leads to her jaw being smashed into the side table.

Kristen is reaching ecstasy and twists her left hand deep into the light gray mock, lifting her foe and freeing her right fist to send two more vicious blows to an unprotected face. With each punch, dark hair flies about, and a small cut becomes visible near her cheek.

Meanwhile, in the parking lot of J Gilbert's Restaurant, Roger and Brad sit fidgeting in a running car, waiting for Roger's phone to repower. Roger curses his ineptitude for allowing the phone battery to deplete. He should have been there for Diane. Neither of the occupants of the car has any clue as to Diane's whereabouts. Their only hope lies in the lithium-ion battery inside Roger's cell.

In addition to the cut, Diane possesses a blackened left eye, a fat and split lip coupled with a bruised jaw. Marveling at her handiwork, Kristen then sends a roundhouse kick to the agent's already maligned face. The kick literally lifts its target off the floor and drops her to a horizontal position near the sofa where this all began.

Trevor smiles but leaves to take a call in the adjoining room. It is from none other than Sheila Crawford, the NSA Station director in DC. To continue to ingratiate herself with the CIA, she informs the soon-to-be director of the call she received from Myles Warner. Trevor now knows that he has been made, and time is running out.

In the other room, Kristen mounts the battered brunette sitting triumphantly on her chest. She gets comfortable and sends a backhanded slap across already bloody lips. Diane is desperate. The room spins, and she knows her body can't take much more. She stretches her right arm outward, feeling on the floor for anything she can use. At first, she finds nothing, but then she feels the toe of her high heel gripping it tightly. She swings it with all her might, aiming the point at Kristen's temple. The blow stuns her rival, and blood begins to mingle with auburn hair, but Kristen is strong and remains in position until a second blow drops her to her back. Dazed but ever resourceful, she extends her right leg, driving her foot up under Dianes' jaw, and presses her head back into the sofa. The murderess is still the more powerful of the two and still appears to be winning the battle.

In the parking lots, Roger's phone shows enough bars to attempt to power up. He quickly locates the tracer application, and the blue dot signifying Diane's presence is only six minutes away. Relieved at the proximity, they glance positively at each other. Tires spin as the agents make a delayed but hasty attempt to rescue their partner.

Kristen looks to be regaining the momentum, her foot bending the agent's neck back beyond where nature intended. Then suddenly, the spike of Diane's heel lands squarely in the kneecap of her outstretched leg. A cry of anguish echoes through the room, and Kristen lays on the floor clutching her coiled limb.

Diane rises and lumbers to the kitchen, where her jacket and holster are stowed. She removes her Glock and unclips the safety. Now standing over the moaning Dryden girl, Diane points it at her head.

"Time to pay up, you little freak. I have waited ten years to find my parents' killers rehearsing every day exactly what I would do at that moment. You destroyed a loving family. You are an evil, ruthless bitch, and now you're going to pay."

At that very moment, a car noise is heard in the driveway. The sound of the front door shattering under the will of Roger Edwards echoes through the room. Roger and Brad rush forward, guns drawn. They find Diane staring trance-like, her pistol focused on a person lying on the floor.

"Diane, stop! Please don't do this," yells her partner.

"This little bitch slaughtered my parents, Roger; she killed them with her bare hands."

"Listen to me, Diane, she will pay. Don't do anything stupid. Justice will be served. I promise you. Don't lower yourself to her level."

"I want her dead."

"Diane, think of what your parents would do now. They were devoted to the law and our justice system. They would want you to honor it as well. Don't throw your career away. You can carry on in their footsteps."

Agent Vitullo closes her eyes with the weapon shaking in her hands.

"Please, Diane, she isn't worth it."

The trigger is squeezed, and the gun fires. A bullet strikes the floor inches from Kristen's head. She now lies trembling in a puddle of her own urine.

Diane hands the gun to Roger, "I guess I'll have to settle for that." She then collapses into his powerful arms, a victim of total exhaustion. Roger ushers Diane to the sofa, she is shuddering uncontrollably. He tries to provide some stability for her bruised body and shattered identity to cling to. Her world is spiraling like a tumultuous eddy. She holds on tight, grateful for his support, but all she can think about right now is getting back to Dr. William Parisi. Brad searched for ice in the small refrigerator, and they chose one of Diane's many injuries to treat.

The police and paramedics are called, and the scene is soon secured. Flashing lights fill the driveway and street. The neighborhood is searched, but there is no sign of Trevor Hawthorne.

Despite Roger and the paramedics' repeated efforts to get her to a hospital, Diane refuses, opting to pull out her cell phone and call the one person who can provide her with some refuge from the events that just transpired. He only relents because he knows there is only one cure for the psychological wounds she received tonight. That cure can only be administered by Dr. Parisi.

He answers. "Hello".

"Is it too late to stop by?"

"Diane, I gave you the key to eliminate that question."

"Great, I really need to see you."

Brad requests that an APB be put out for Trevor Hawthorne. It appears tomorrow's confirmation will be postponed indefinitely. They knew he was present in the house and questioned Diane on the approximate time of his departure.

Before contacting Myles in Chicago, Roger stares into Dianes' eyes, desperately checking on her mental status. She stares back, putting forth a painful grin at her partner.

"Roger, thank you. I really owe you for everything, but can you take it from here?"

His look says it all. No more words are needed. Having found someone, he fully understands why she wants to be with the doctor tonight. After all, if she needs attention, who better to provide it?

"Diane, you did the right thing. Are you sure you're ok? I can't leave you if you're not."

"To be honest, Roger, this hurts more than anything I have ever felt. That includes the news of my parents' death. At least then, I made a vow to find the murderers, and it kept me going. Something to blot out the sadness. This is really hard."

"You have a bright career and possibly a real good man. That's a lot to live for. Keep the faith."

"Once again, you are my rock. Thank you for being there, Roger." They embrace.

Brad offers to drive Diane to Dr. Parisi's residence.

Meanwhile, Roger calls Myles in Chicago to advise him that Diane is okay and Kristen is in custody. He also must tell him that Trevor has vanished. The Director then groans, the biggest sigh of relief possible for a man his size.

This has been a painful night for Agent Vitullo, both physically and mentally. She never considered the consequences could to so enormous. The emotional repercussions she suffered dwarfed any professional satisfaction. While content with the knowledge that the crime had been solved the revelation that her "Uncle" and "Stepfather" was the culprit was way too challenging to grasp. That would indeed require the healing that only time could provide.

She did manage to take some solace at the sight of her psychopathic "stepsister" and serial murderer handcuffed and perp walking through the safe house in her soiled tights. But it was a small consolation. How close she came to pulling the trigger was a question no one could answer.

Chapter 54

Friday 2:00 AM, Gallery 64 Apartments, 64 H Street, Washington, DC

It's after 2:00 AM when Brad's car stops in front of the Gallery 64 Apartments on H Street. Diane thanks him for the ride, the rescue, and the ice pack. Moving gingerly, she exits the car. Her body aches, but that pain pales in comparison to the hurt in her heart. Roger told her Myles wanted them both to report to the DC office at noon tomorrow. She fills Brad in.

"I may get a medal or a pink slip. Both outcomes are equally possible."

"You did great, Diane. I am proud to know you."

"How come I don't feel so good, but thank you, Brad. You did pretty good yourself. We will call you after the meeting."

The walk to the elevator seemed much longer than it did just yesterday. Diane leans against the back wall as the car rises. If this was a victory, it certainly didn't feel like one. The detective was beaten up physically, mentally, and emotionally. She carries her heels in one hand, using the other to press the icepack to her cheek. Her destination is the only positive thing left in her life. The one remaining safe harbor in a life sent adrift. She finally arrives at the apartment and begins to insert the key into the lock when the door opens. Will is standing there to grab her tightly and hug her. She falls meekly into his caress.

Not a word is spoken.

He lifts her off her feet and carries her to the sofa, where she lays her head in his lap while he strokes her hair.

"Everything is going to be okay, Diane."

It's not long before the soothing motion of his hand has her in dreamland. Her sleep is both restful and seemingly eternal. His soft touch brings her the only comfort felt on a day of shattered dreams. Reconciling the recent revelations will take months, if not years, to resolve. She is ever grateful that Will has entered her life in this most critical time. The ghosts of Trevor and Kristen will not be exorcised anytime soon. She curses the vow she has made to find her parents' killers. How could she know it would lead back to the man who raised her after they passed? Her eyelids grow heavy, and they finally close.

The next thing she remembers is the bright morning light shining through the window. Will is sitting under her in the same position as the night prior. She just stares at him until he stirs. He stayed with her on the sofa the entire night so as not to disturb her slumber.

"How about you get a nice warm shower while I make breakfast?"

"Sounds wonderful."

Diane emerges from the shower clad in "her" robe. Both sit, knowing they are faced with a major problem now that the case is all but closed. That problem is geography. Soon, Diane will need to return to Chicago, where she is based. The young agent is torn between the only two stable pillars left in her life.

They discuss various options as both want the liaison to continue. None of the alternatives appear to be viable, but they vow to work out a solution that both can live with. Diane's injuries prevent any amorous activities, but the doctor sees nothing that won't heal quickly. Breakfast lingers for hours, and Diane recounts how the evening and her past mingled. They discuss assorted options for the relationship, but no real solution is found. At 11:15 AM, Diane notices the time and remembers that Myles had summoned them for a meeting at noon.

"I need to get to the DC office in forty-five minutes. Can we resume this discussion later?"

"I'll put as much time into this as you want, Diane."

She rushes to the bedroom and returns in her jeans and Georgetown sweatshirt, only this time with more appropriate footwear. They embrace, kissing passionately.

As she departs, both are somewhat somber and frightened that they will not be able to overcome the outside forces conspiring to separate their lives. They have forty-eight hours to reach an accord.

Chapter 55

Friday 12:00 PM, NSA Headquarters, Undisclosed location, Washington, DC

The agents both show up at the appointed time. They notice an extremely elevated level of activity. It seems like people are bustling about every inch of the building. They also noticed three of the top NSA brass were present. Everyone is in a serious mood.

Each entered the office thinking that the primary focus of the day would be an intense debriefing. Each new time, they were going to face tough questions, and every action they took would be scrutinized to the maximum level possible. Both know they broke some rules and that they were vulnerable to the ramifications thereof.

"Well, Roger, are we getting praised or punished?"

"The Vegas line is even money."

He always knew what to say to brighten the mood.

The agents cringe when they see Myles ushered into Sheila Crawford's office with two District Directors. This was more serious than expected. Bringing him into DC to meet the top dogs couldn't be a good thing.

"I may have gotten him into big trouble."

They see an animated conversation through the window and hear voices raised to the height of an auctioneer. It is a very heated discussion. Arms flail, and a fist is pounded into a desk. To say the meeting was contentious would be a gross understatement.

"Poor Myles. That bitch never did like me. She is going to make him pay."

"We are really screwed," adds Roger.

Just when it appears that the worst-case scenario is about to unfold, the two Senior personnel walk around the desk and cuff Sheila Crawford. One leads her out of the office. The glare she gives Diane on her way past could melt an iceberg. The other asks Myles to sit, and they engage in what appears to be serious discussions. Another intense conversation ensues making the agents wait drag on exponentially.

"Oh no, now it's his turn." Diane tries not to look.

There seems to be a lot of give and take happening inside the office. Myles is talking as much as listening. Then, the Regional Director rises and leaves the office with Myles sitting in Sheila's desk chair. He remains still doing nothing for several minutes. This adds more tension to the two agents waiting outside to learn their fate. The common term to describe the moment would be "sweating bullets."

After several moments, they are waived into the small room. They enter hesitantly and sit in front of the man, awaiting judgment.

"Hello, agents."

"Boss," they reply in unison, their tone hushed.

Diane manages a faint, "What's up?"

"Well, Diane, it seems that you have a talent for making enemies."

"Sir?"

"Let me finish."

"I called Director Crawford last night when I learned your uncle Trevor was indeed the force behind this operation. She absolutely refused to lift a finger to help you or me, for that matter. The bitch proceeded to hang the phone up on me, leaving one of my agents in jeopardy. That really ticked me off. Refusing to help an agent in trouble, even you, is a cardinal sin. I was so angry I initiated a search of her phone records. It appears she telephoned Trevor last night while he was at the safe house. She was trying to schmooze with the new Director of the CIA. The call tipped him off to my awareness and afforded him the ability to escape. We believe she was the leak all along. Seems like the big boys took serious offense to that, as you saw from her new shiny bracelets."

"Sorry, Myles, we didn't know any of this went down. Are you ok?"

"I am not sure, agents. I've got a lot of thinking to do. To make a long story short, due to Ms. Crawford's demise, I was offered a transfer to DC and the Directorship here."

Both Roger and Diane express their congratulations and relief. "Congrats, chief, what did you tell them?" spouts Edwards. "You really deserve this."

"I said I would accept on one and only one condition."

Diane screams, "You're killing us, boss."

"I would take the job if my two best agents agreed to relocate here with me."

Roger and Diane looked at each other in utter shock. In an instant, their mutual problem with geography vanished. Was this a dream?

Both agents gleefully accept the prospect of relocating to Washington, DC. There was immediate relief in each of their hearts.

"I know I am going to regret this," the new DC Director grumbles. "The only thing that stands to benefit here is my ulcer."

Diane replies, "You probably will, sir."

"Now, let's go to lunch to celebrate. I would like to get something spicy to eat while I still have a stomach."

The agents stare at each other before Roger nods and Diane speaks. "Give us ten minutes, sir. We each have a quick call to make."

Made in United States
Troutdale, OR
09/10/2025

34426452R00156